Beyond
the Mango Tree

Beyond the Mango Tree

By Amy Bronwen Zemser

 Greenwillow Books, New York

Page 12: The phrase "Bone at my bone" is from "Unknown Girl in the Maternity Ward" by Anne Sexton (from *To Bedlam and Part Way Back*, 1960).

Pages 46–47: Excerpts are from "The Nameless One" by James Clarence Mangan (first published in the *Irishman*, 1849).

Page 138: The phrase "golden lightning" is from "To a Skylark" by Percy Bysshe Shelley (from *Prometheus Unbound*, 1820). The phrase "discover stars, and sail in the wind's eye" is from Canto X of *Don Juan* by George Gordon, Lord Byron (1823).

The text of this book was set in Trump.
Printed in the United States of America
First Edition   10 9 8 7 6 5 4 3 2 1

Library of Congress Cataloging-in-Publication Data

Zemser, Amy Bronwen.
   Beyond the mango tree / by Amy Bronwen Zemser.
      p.   cm.
   Summary: While living in Liberia with her possessive, diabetic mother and often-absent father, twelve-year-old Sarina longs for a friend with whom to experience the world beyond her yard.
ISBN 0-688-16005-0   [1. Mothers and daughters—Fiction.
2. Diabetes—Fiction.   3. Liberia—Fiction.   4. Friendship—Fiction.]   I. Title.   PZ7.Z424Be 1998
[Fic]—dc21   97-32268   CIP   AC

For my mother, Annette,
and my father, Alan

Africa is painted in my mind

Contents

Beyond
the Mango Tree

CHAPTER 1

Tied to a Tree

The earth is red in Africa. It is rainy season, and water rushes in streams, rapidly filling the hollow dips along the rust-colored roads, causing them to overflow. These are not like the shallow rain puddles I am accustomed to in Boston. These are African rain puddles, deep and soaked with mud the color of crumbled bricks. These pools of water frighten me because, in the face of steady rain, they have no time to empty.

And I am left here, in the rain, tied to a tree. The water level rises, above my naked feet, past my ankles, and I am wondering now: What lies beneath the water's surface? I do not like to think about it.

My mother has tied me here because I left the yard today. I did not go far. I never do. I was not gone long. I never am. But my mother wants me to stay with her always, because I am her only daughter. Because she needs me.

She often ties me here, to this tree, because she needs me. She doesn't leave me here very long, and she is always sorry afterward, when the *reaction*, as she calls it, has passed. She will say, "I am sorry, Sarina. I don't remember what happened." And then she will untie me from the tree and there will be a space in time, a period of days perhaps, when there are no reactions. And then soon enough she will forget to eat, or perhaps to take her insulin, and she will fear that I will leave her once again. And so I will once more be anchored to a tree, or the fence, or a chair even, while raindrops drench my clothes and hair, moistening my tongue inside a mouth that will open to form the word—

"Mama!"

She hurries down the sopping path today, carrying the scissors—my captor, my savior—that she will use to cut me loose from the same twine she earlier wrapped in tight circles around me.

When she reaches me, she places one finger beneath my chin and tilts my face to hers. I look into her clear gray eyes and see that her reaction has not ended. Her sugar levels have dropped even lower, and she moves awkwardly, without precision. She moves to untie me, but her hands are shaking and she drops the scissors. They slide into a puddle at my feet. I can feel them, cold against my toes.

"Don't worry," I say. "They're right here. Just reach down."

"Oh," she says. She is confused, and stares into the rushing water. "The scissors . . . I've dropped them."

She is fading fast. Think. Don't go, Mom, not now. Cut me loose first. Then I will do whatever you say. I'll lead you to the house. I'll help you into the bed. Just reach for the scissors. They are right here!

But my mother shakes her head and backs away, frightened by the things she cannot see.

"Please don't leave me here," I say, but I know she cannot hear me. She cannot even hear herself. She is somewhere beyond the yard, above the trees, floating in the quiet spaces between silver drops of rain. I watch her drift up the path and into our house. I strain to hear the sound of the door closing.

I move my toes and feel the loop of the cold scissors handle. Sometimes I can make the rain stop if I think of pleasant things. I wonder about Te Te, our housekeeper, away at the market today. Will she buy a soursop fruit? Thomas Scott, the cook, will fix collard greens and chicken tonight, after he rouses from his afternoon nap. I will watch him quarter and debone the chicken. He will set the rice to boil and then begin slicing the peppers for a salad. How long does it take for rice to finish steaming? Will the peppers be green or yellow? I am still envisioning my way through dinner when I am suddenly interrupted by voices.

A group of very young Liberian children is gathering around me to stare. How strange I must look to them, a twelve-year-old white girl tied to a tree just inside the gate to her large brick home. They look at me, their eyes opened wide with curiosity. Their clothing is wet and torn, and their feet are bare, but they are smiling. I think they look friendly, and if I were not bound to this tree, then I might play with them.

One brave child ventures forth and touches

4

me. He runs a finger down the top of my head, along my rain-sodden hair, and then detours across the bridge of my nose. There, he rests for a moment. I wonder what he is thinking. Abruptly, he pinches me.

"Ow!" I yell, scowling. "That hurt!" Suddenly they all spring upon me, prodding my face with small, exploring fingers. They poke at me with their toes. One pinches my leg.

"Stop it!" I shout, twisting uselessly within my constraints. But I am small for my age and cannot free myself, so the children descend upon me like a cloud of hovering fruit flies. They hurt my pride more than my body, but still I cry out at them.

An older boy appears. He speaks harshly to them in a language I do not understand. Magically, they disperse and scatter down the muddy path.

"Thanks," I say, although I am too angry to smile.

The boy does not answer me. Instead, he stares quizzically at the knots of twine that hold me firmly against the bark of the tree. He stares at the flesh on my arm that has turned a peculiar bluish color against the tightened twine. He

5

reaches out and gently touches a knot. A noise escapes his lips. A grunt.

"There are scissors."

He looks at me.

"Scissors," I tell him, motioning downward with my head, toward the pool of orange-red rainwater swirling around my ankles.

The boy kneels beside me and lowers his hands into the rainwater. His arms are thin and seem to disappear inside the dark pool. Rain drips from his eyelids as he stirs the water, creating a wave of circular patterns. His dark hands, unlike my own pale feet, do not seem to twitch in fear of the unseen bottom.

Within moments he finds the scissors and I am free. I am about to say thank you—thank you so very much for saving me from the earth and the water and the merciless rain, and what is your name and how old are you anyhow and did you know that I don't really have any friends here except for Katrina and she is only six—when I hear a shrill sound. It is the sound of a voice, and that voice belongs to my mother.

CHAPTER 2

A Boy Called Boima

"**W**hat's your name?" I ask the boy quickly, because I know I do not have much time. His clothes are soaked and torn, barely covering his reedy figure. Bones protrude in places where on my own body I must press down on flesh to feel them.

"*Sarina!*"

"I," he says, grinning and pointing to himself, "Boima." His voice is low and soft, as if he does not want to interrupt the insect's walk upon the guava leaf.

"*Sarina!*"

"I'm Sarina," I say, feeling slightly foolish.

"Sarina," Boima repeats slowly, as if he must

pronounce it correctly the first time. His voice is pure, like yellow sunlight.

"Sarina, where are you?"

"I have to go," I say.

Boima nods. "You ma, she callin'."

"Yeah. Do you live near me? Maybe I could visit you sometime."

"Sarina!"

"I livin' pas' Ol' Road, Chugbor way. Mornin' time I workin' Joe Ba'. Ehn't you know Joe Ba'?"

"The market," I say. I have heard of it.

"Yeh. I sellin' basket for my ma. You come there sometime. I can show you all kind a something-o." Boima ends his sentence with an emphatic *oh!*, customary Liberian English.

My mother is walking down the path. Now the rain has stopped.

"Okay," I tell him. "I'll come sometime." I am thinking, Te Te goes to market every day. Maybe she will take me to Joe Bar, wherever it is.

Boima's brown eyes move past me then, to follow the hibiscus bush along the path, beyond a low-growing papaya tree, to where my mother stands. She is fair skinned and light eyed, very pretty. Her dress is simple, palest yellow, and to Boima I imagine that she must look like a spirit, as light and delicate as the wind itself. He proffers up a little smile, warm and hopeful. She does not smile back.

"Sarina, please ask him to leave," she says, not very quietly. My mother has not yet grasped that most Liberians speak a dialect of English. Boima understands her.

"I don't want to. He was kind to me."

"We don't know him," she says. She looks neither at me nor at Boima, preferring to view the shady green mango tree that powerfully embraces our overgrown yard. The twine, now in pieces, floats in a pool of rainwater at the base of the tree. But my mother does not ask how I came to be untied. She does not remember tying me to the tree in the first place.

I turn to say good-bye to Boima, but he has already gone. I lock my teeth in place, hard, and walk up toward the house.

"Please rinse your feet, Sarina," my mother says, following me up the path. "You don't want to bring chiggers into the house."

Chiggers are mites that live in the sand. If you walk outside without shoes, a chigger may burrow deep inside your toe and lay an egg beneath the nail. Once my mother had a chigger that left an egg under the cuticle of her little toe. She did not even know it was there until her foot became swollen and inflamed. Thomas Scott took a very sharp needle to the raw skin while my mother's face moved in pain and horror. When he held the egg up on the end of the needle, I could see how big it was, the size of an apple seed, bone white.

My mother screamed when she saw that egg and immediately went into physical reaction. It was as if an electrical current had jumped through her veins, twisting her limbs in frightful contortions. Her whole body became a live wire, jerking on the kitchen floor until Thomas Scott was forced to hold her against the pantry door while I pressed a cup of juice to her lips.

As I rinse my feet I think about the chigger incident. That was eight months ago, just after we first moved to Liberia. I think my mother's light faded away that afternoon. From then on, she stopped seeing me and forgot how to take care of herself. My mother has to pay very close attention to her body. She must take insulin when her sugar is high, or eat or drink when it is low. But here, away from her doctoral students and her colleagues and her dissertations, she has only books, and me, to remind her of the life she left behind. My father does not know this, or perhaps he does not have time to notice, since he is often away at the lumber camps in Nimba County. He only knows that I am smart and can take care of things while he is away. I always have, although I do not always want to.

"Did you rinse all of the mud?" my mother asks. She is standing right behind me.

"Yes. I'm going in to change now."

Inside the house, my body is instantly chilled by the force of air fueled by the air conditioners. Because my mother's body temperature is naturally high, she loathes the tropical heat and so keeps the indoors very cold. Te Te and Thomas Scott wear sweaters whenever they work inside.

In my bedroom I unfold a crisp green sundress, carefully ironed into an even square of cloth and placed upon my bed by Te Te. When I am dry and dressed, with hair combed, I go to my mother, to make sure that she is all right. I find her sitting neatly in a straight-backed chair in the front room. An open book rests upon her lap. She stares straight ahead, looking at nothing, waiting for me. When she sees me she holds out her arms.

"I'm glad you remembered to drink juice," I say, thinking of her earlier, by the tree, in the rain.

"Thomas Scott helped me."

"Oh."

"'Bone at my bone,'" she whispers, quoting from somewhere as she pulls me close to her. "You are mine only, I cannot share you with anyone. Do you understand? What would I do without you?" She presses my cheek to hers and holds it there. From the kitchen I can hear Thomas Scott chopping collard greens. I can smell chicken cooking in the pot. I think about a boy called Boima. I feel happy.

CHAPTER 3

Whippers
and Choppers

"**W**hy you want go Joe Ba'?" Oldman Jacob asks me early the next morning from where he has been sitting, all night long, in his smooth wooden chair. Jacob is our night watchman. We call him Oldman as a sign of respect.

I shrug. The perfumed scent of Oldman's pipe tobacco gently permeates the air. "I just want to go. I've never been."

"Small-small Kwi Ma want go for big-big Joe Ba'." Oldman laughs and crosses one long leg over the other. "Wha' you askin' me 'bout that place there?"

Oldman Jacob is tall and clean, with soft gray hair. He wears a brown woolen sweater and chews the bitter pink kola nut. Beside his chair

he keeps two weapons, a stiff black whip fash-
ioned out of wire and hard plastic, and a silver
cutlass with a wooden handle. He calls these
tools of his trade his "whipper" and his "chopper" respectively, and never seems to tire of
relating stories that detail the many uses of
these weapons during skirmishes with the
rogues who sometimes sneak into the yards of
American homes.

"How big is Joe Bar?" I ask him now. "What
do they sell there?"

"Everything they get to the place." Oldman
wraps his smooth fingers around the bowl of his
pipe and removes it from his mouth. "They get
five-cent groun' pea an' they get kola nut. They
get benniseed an' groun' nut and palm nut an'
coconut—"

"A lot of nuts."

"Yeh. An' they get nyama nyama thing, jes'
like—"

"What's nyama nyama?"

"That different-different thing, like hairpin,
comb, key chain, razor blade and so. They get
hongry rice an' chickle'. The woman them sellin' orange, pawpaw an' banana, two dolla', three
dolla', too sweet-o. You can find bitter ball an'

potato greens. They get eddo an' boney. Everything you want jes' line up on the table there. An' under the table you can see too many small boy jes' talkin' something an' jabbin' with they friend. Joe Ba', that good-good place-o. Get plenty for see."

Oldman Jacob leans back and rests one elbow on the arm of the wooden chair. He is pleased with his description of Joe Bar and so replaces his pipe between his teeth with a satisfied click. Blue-gray smoke dissipates slowly into the warm air of early morning.

"Oldman Jacob?"

"Yeh."

"Can you take me there?"

"Wha' place?"

"Joe Bar. What do you think?"

"No, Kwi Ma. I not able it."

"Why not? I'll buy you some tobacco if you want. I've got five dollars."

But Oldman snorts amicably and waves me away with one arm. "Lemme be now, Kwi Ma. I not get time for market business. I workin' man. Go carry you own self to the place."

"But I don't even know where it is!"

"Kwi Ma, ehn't you see this?"

"Stop calling me that."

"Wha'?"

"Kwi Ma. I don't like it." *Kwi* is the Liberian English word for civilized, for someone who can read books.

"I say, Kwi—I mean, small gal, ehn't you see this?" Oldman repeats, holding up his cutlass for me to admire.

"I told you, I see it. Please take me to Joe Bar, Oldman."

"Now, this thing here—"

"It's a big knife. I know. You've told me a hundred times—"

"This thing ain' no knife." Oldman looks disappointed, as if he had failed to educate me well. "This my chopper own. Rogue comin', krick krick in the night, I be takin' my whipper and my chopper an' I will catch that man-o. I can whip he back an' I can cut he neck, no time, my friend. But I got to keep all my eye on the groun', in the tree, behind the house. I got to do my walk 'bout the grass. From the night to comin' the day, I got to stay behind my own self. Ehn't you see, I too busy, you gal, too busy tryin' to juke the bad man who doin' bad-bad something. I ain' get time for small-small gal. I

16

say, go find your own way to reach Joe Ba'. I workin' man. I a workin' man-o!''

While Oldman Jacob slices the air with his silver cutlass, lost in battle with foes of nights past, the kitchen screen door drawls out a whine and slams shut behind Te Te. She looks from Oldman to me the way a movie camera would pan a wide angle, long and slow and deliberate. Oldman returns to his wooden chair, but I do not move.

"Sarina, you humbuggin' this man?" Her question is directed at me, but she looks to Oldman for the answer.

"No," I reply, before Oldman has the chance to speak.

"Why you not doin' school study?" she asks. "Already you done?"

"No," I say, hoping my eyes are the steel gray color of Oldman's cutlass. "I don't want to study by myself anymore today." The fine hairs along my back stiffen, and I feel curved inside, like an angry cat about to hiss. I hate the dull correspondence course pages I must complete every day. My mother does not like the American school in Monrovia, so I learn by myself, at home.

"How much you do?" Te Te asks.

"Two pages. Want to check?" The liquid meanness of this question pulses hotly through my veins. I feel powerful. Te Te has never learned to read.

If Te Te is affected by this insult to her humanity, she does not make it known. Instead, she presses her lips together and fixes a narrow stare upon me. She knows as well as I that a silent war rages between us, a war without language. I stare right back at her dark eyes and think of wood. Hard wood.

"Plenty palava." Oldman Jacob shifts his feet and snorts again. His voice cracks our silence like hot water on ice. *Palaver* means discussion, or argument.

Te Te hands me a shopping list, written in my mother's script, and turns her back to me. She is neatly dressed in a light red kwi dress, probably purchased at Waterside, a downtown open market on Water Street. She is small, but firmly rooted and powerful.

"Make market with me, read my paper," she says, looking out at the mango tree in the yard. It is not a request, but a command.

While I scan the list of fruits my mother needs

to eat to raise her sugar levels, Te Te argues with Oldman about the price of boney fish.

"Wha' you talkin', boney. Ehn't you know you ain' get money for that one there? Boney too dear."

"That me waste my money? Time Sunday reach, my whole village fini askin' me for five cent here, ten cent there."

"That you eat the money, Oldman. Then you cry poor mouth for rest o' the month an' got to ask Bossman to credit you five dolla' every time."

"I not eat all my money-o," Oldman insists, sucking his teeth at Te Te's accusation that money burns a hole in his pocket.

I am only half listening to the argument. In my mind, a plan is taking shape, weaving itself into words that will resonate with far more importance than the high price of boney fish.

"Te Te," I say, taking a slow deep breath. "This paper says . . . I mean, my mother wants us to try a different market today. She thinks that fruit may be cheaper at"—I squint at the paper, feigning indifference—"Joe Bar." I hope my voice has not trembled.

"Joe Ba'?" Te Te looks surprised, remotely confused.

"Maybe my mother thinks Charlotte's Supermarket is getting too expensive," I say. My heart knocks against my rib cage. Most Americans shop at Charlotte's Supermarket, because it is small and clean, and has air conditioning.

Oldman is silent. But I can see his eyes through the rising clouds of tobacco smoke. He is staring at me.

"Wha' you talkin', small gal?" Te Te says, perhaps attempting to unearth me from the great lie that I have told. But I am determined to hold my ground.

"The paper says that fruits are cheaper there," is all I say. I have no idea if this is really true. I am taking a dangerous risk, although I also have an advantage. No one, not even Thomas Scott, challenges my mother.

Te Te snaps the shopping list away from me. Her eyebrows form a *V* in concentrated effort to discern the lettering of my mother's scrawling hand.

"This paper say to reach to Joe Ba'?"

"Yes." Some ants are marching along the cracks in the stone veranda tile. The creases in the hemline of my dress are wrinkled. I make a silent prayer to God.

"Joe Ba' too dirty," Te Te says, and opens the screen door just enough to reach inside for the market basket, which hangs on a wooden peg above the counter.

Oldman Jacob still looks at me. I look back at him but do not speak. Instead, I think of the pointed black rock in the African ocean, unswayed by giant furling waves and rolling foam. I am as unyielding as the rock.

Oldman Jacob takes his pipe out of his mouth. His eyes know many things.

"Bring me big-big kola nut, you gal," is all he says.

CHAPTER 4

Joe Bar

The heels of my thongs snap and catch onto the back of my dress, making it difficult for me to keep up with Te Te's even strides along the path. She pushes ahead of me without speaking and does not look back to see how far I lag behind. I think she would not care if I blended into the still air and red earth of Liberia and disappeared forever. This thought infuriates me. After all, Te Te is our housekeeper and I am her responsibility. She is supposed to care if I live or die, I reason, and so shout, "Slow down!"

"Gal draggin' shoe. Ain' get restin' time. Got to reach home befo' you ma wake up."

My mother usually sleeps until noon. When she awakens, she is often unpleasant, and in need of a meal. For a moment I see my mother with the eye that looks inside my mind. She is pale, with hands that flutter like an awkward fledgling, restless and agitated. I close that eye and look around me, at blue sky, at yellow sun, at green hibiscus plants dotted with red flowers. Some Liberians stare at us as we march along the path. I feel self-conscious and clumsy, like a puppy struggling to keep up with the determined gait of its master.

"Stop leavin' tail behind," Te Te scolds, but I like to watch the people as we go. Men carry one-hundred-pound bags of rice over their shoulders as if they were feather pillows. Children run along the dusty road, rolling an old soccer ball or an abandoned car tire. But to me, the tall Liberian women are the most elegant. Many balance large baskets on their heads, their colorful *lappahs*, or dress cloths, trailing regally behind them. Some need extra yards of lappah to wrap around the infants sleeping cozily against their backs.

Sometimes, although I would never tell anyone this, I like to imagine myself growing smaller and smaller until I too am an infant once more, molded into a warm oval shape against a mother who will hold me to the steady circular beat of her heart. This mother will be tall and strong and filled with love that is not born of desperation, or sickness, or need. This mother will care for her daughter in the way that is meant to be—

"Sarina!" Te Te has stopped walking suddenly, and I collide with her on the path. I look up and see that a gardener named Flomo has paused to chat. Although we are in a hurry, it would be considered rude for Te Te to pass by without first saying hello.

"How you keepin'?" Te Te asks Flomo, who chews a toothpick and grins broadly at me.

"Jes' tryin'," he says. "Where you reachin' to?"

"Joe Bar," I tell him. "We need fruit."

"Joe Ba'," Flomo exclaims, as if I had just handed him a small wrapped present. "You will see plenty thing-o!"

Flomo climbs coconut trees. I have seen him wave to me from in between the shiny leaves before sending down a shower of thudding coconuts.

"Where are *you* going?" I ask him.

"Breslo family, for garden."

"Oh."

"You gal," Flomo says, shifting his toothpick from one side of his mouth to the other with his tongue, "Ehn't you know that small-small Breslo gal get monkey?"

"Katrina got a monkey? When?"

"Huntin' man come two days befo' from upcountry. He fine shot two down, *bam*, jes' like that, and baby fall from the tree. That baby cry too much-o. Loss he ma."

My heart aches to see the baby monkey. I look at Te Te, but her face bears no expression. She lifts the straps of the market basket up higher on her shoulder.

"Flomo, can't you take me to see that monkey sometime?"

"Yes. No. Maybe so," Flomo jokes, and says something to Te Te that I do not understand. Both Flomo and Te Te speak *Kpelle*, one of the local languages of Liberia. Te Te's face opens into soft laughter when she talks with Flomo, which hollows my insides.

"What's so funny?" I demand to know.

"That nothin', small gal," Flomo says, still laughing. "Jes I never see white gal who tie she face so. That you never smile."

"I smile sometimes," I mumble, drawing a line in the dirt with my thong. I look up at Flomo. "I'll smile if you take me to see that monkey. I promise I will!"

But Flomo just laughs again as Te Te nods good-bye and continues down the path.

"I promise I won't tie my face," I call, walking backward, still facing Flomo, who moves off in the opposite direction, his gardening shears balanced crazily on his shoulder. "I promise I'll smile!"

I can still hear the echo of Flomo's laughter as Te Te and I round the bend toward Joe Bar.

"Mind me," Te Te warns, when we are standing outside the market a few minutes later. Joe Bar looks nothing like I imagined. It is huge and teeming with activity, a great circular construction with a corrugated tin roof flimsily held up by thick wooden poles. Inside it is filled with loud voices and unappealing smells.

"Two for five, two for five chickle'."

"Ehn't you want buy my groun' pea?"

"Gbapleh fish, fine-fine gbapleh fish!"

Liberian women sit alongside their wares in a strange mix of assorted goods, squirming children and bare feet. The air is moist and still,

redolent of milk left too long in the sun, fish
left too long out of the ocean. I am uncomfortable here but eager to find Boima. I follow closely
behind Te Te, almost but not quite touching
her as the throngs of marketgoers push us along
in a damp wave of heat and moving bodies. We
pass many tables, some brightly adorned with
piles of candies in pinks and greens and blues,
others offering a mix of goods, such as leather
bracelets, shoe polish, cheap plastic sandals, and
hair oil. When we reach the fruit tables, Te Te
silently hands me the shopping list and I read
it out to her.

"How much fo' green pawpaw?" Te Te asks
a woman seated on a table next to papayas,
bananas, guavas, and butter-pears. A sleeping
baby leans against her, its head flopped sideways
across its chest. Flies buzz and settle on its eye-
lid. I look away.

"One dolla' fo' that one there."

"An' pineapple?"

"Two dolla'."

"How much fo' banana?"

"One dolla' fifty cent, bunch. Lady, you want
it?" Te Te inspects a guava and turns up her
nose.

"Get good guava, this," the woman says.

"Look spoil to me."

"Spoil? Wha' you talkin'? You playin' sabi with me?"

"Fante man never say he boney rotten," Te Te says dryly, ignoring the woman's accusation that she is playing *sabi*, or being stingy. "I give you fifty cent fo' pawpaw."

"Fifty cent fo' pawpaw," the woman cries. "You sabi woman fo' true-o!"

"An' I give you one dolla' fifty cent fo' pineapple, that my last price. . . ."

While Te Te bargains for fruit, I take a few steps away, hoping to spot Boima at a nearby table. Instead, I find a thin old man carefully setting down harmonicas in shiny silver rows. His hands move slowly, methodically, but when he sees me he plucks a harmonica from the bunch and blows into it. An odd tune forces its way into the air. I smile and shake my head at him. I look back at Te Te, but she is still contesting the price of a soursop and so I wander a little farther on.

Once accustomed to the rank air of Joe Bar, I decide that Oldman is right. The market is boiling with activity. I stop at another table covered with mounds of cellophane-wrapped pepper-mints.

"Five cent, five cent," a teenage girl calls, but I shake my head again. Where could Boima be in all of this, I wonder. There must be over a hundred tables here. I drift a little more, and then suddenly look back and realize that I can no longer see Te Te amid the crowds. My view is eclipsed by too many people, all carrying market baskets or small children. I rush past a table twitching with half-dead fish, their eyes and mouths wide open at being trawled from the ocean floor. Chickens, bound at the feet and beak, flap pitifully from the next table, their wings jerking in an effort to free themselves. I pause to watch the handing over of dollars and a flash of silver light on an axe blade, but when I hear a funny noise, I look away and hurry on, afraid that I am going to be ill if I do not find my way back to Te Te soon.

I look for her but with every place I turn, my mind and nostrils fill with a terrible sense of dread and panic. Why did I wander away, I ask myself as I rest my hand upon a table's edge. Something furry touches my fingertips. I spin around and find myself staring into the open eyes of a dead monkey. Rows of these awful black heads cover the table, their eyes staring out at nothingness, their pointed teeth visible in what must have been their last expressions before the silver crack and fall of a hunter's blade. I shudder, both horrified and fascinated, but cannot bring myself to look away. Where did these poor monkeys come from? And what were they being sold for?

"I don't like it-o," says a voice from behind me. Boima. I breathe a sigh of relief and wipe the perspiration from the edges of my face.

"I was looking for you," I say. "But I got lost."

"I waitin'." He takes my hand and leads me away from the haunting image of the dead monkeys. "Come see wha' I get."

Boima wends his way through Joe Bar with even grace and speed and does not stop until we reach a table covered with little round baskets, each no larger than my hand, deftly twisted together with brightly colored strands of wire. Boima handles them lovingly, placing a hand gently on top of every one, the way a proud father might introduce his children.

"Did you make all of these?" I ask him, amazed at his handiwork. Each basket is individual and beautiful, a beam of colorful light across the dull wooden table.

"I the one," Boima says proudly.

"They're beautiful," I whisper, unable to lift my gaze from the circular weave of rainbow patterns around and around each basket.

"I sellin' fo' my ma," Boima says. "Every mornin', sellin'. Money fo' rice, money fo' groun' pea."

"Is your ma here?" I ask him, looking around suddenly.

"No. She to the house. I get three small brothers, one big sister."

"Where's your father?"

Boima's face darkens. "My pa has die," he says quietly.

"Oh." There is a silence, and then I say, "I don't have any brothers or sisters." Boima nods and smiles again, the same easy smile that filled me with warmth the day before.

"How long you livin' Liberia?" Boima wants to know.

"Eight months," I tell him.

"Wha' you see, now?"

"What do you mean, what do I see? I see palm trees. I see the rain and the dirt road."

"No, I say, where you been?"

I shrug. "My mother's sick a lot. And my father works upcountry most of the time, so . . ."

Boima's eyebrows raise adventurously. "I can take you to see different-different thing. Me part, I know Monrovia too good-o. I can show you the cityside an' the sea. I know from Duport Road to the Bong Mine Bridge. Liberia all right-o."

I feel electric. "You mean you could take me to those places?" I ask. "To the ocean and the downtown city streets?"

"Ocean lagoon that green, like you slipper," Boima says, pointing to the thongs on my feet.

"Maybe you could come to my house tomorrow," I say, lifting one foot and then setting it down again. "In the afternoon, after you get done selling—"

"Sarina!" Te Te appears then, parting the crowds with a long and powerful arm. She is a wave of unspeakable fury.

"Oh," I whisper. How long had I been away from her? A minute? An hour?

"You fini run from me?" Te Te's fingers press down to the bone of my arm and she glances sideways at Boima for less than a second before jerking me away.

". . . runnin' roun' lookin' for you like chicken with no head. I comin' tell you ma, you make me vex too much . . ."

I turn my body as far around as it will go before Te Te's grip can twist my arm from the socket. Boima follows swiftly behind and presses something into my free hand.

"Ocean blue, like you eye," he says, and falls back into the crowds. I squint until I cannot see him anymore.

Out in the fresh air and sun once again, I take to the road with Te Te. She is as weighted down with anger as I am floating up with joy. We rush past flimsy cardboard signs advertising Guinness stout and Coca-Cola and still Te Te does not speak to me, not even to remind me to hurry up. Around and around on my finger I swing the basket that Boima has given me. It is the color of the ocean, the color of my eyes. I wish Flomo could see me from his coconut treetop. Then he would know my face is filled with smiles.

CHAPTER 5

Why Is for
the Yellow Bird

The next day I awaken early, feeling light and filled with air. Boima will be here in the afternoon. I slide out from beneath my covers and walk barefoot down the cold marble hallway toward the kitchen, where I can hear Thomas Scott washing dishes and arguing with Oldman.

"Wha' you want two woman fo'?" Oldman is asking Thomas Scott from behind the screen door. His silhouette is centered neatly in the doorway, like a portrait in a picture frame. "Ehn't you know one wife that too many—plenty woman that palava-o!"

"I got to do it." Thomas Scott lifts a wet dish from the sink and places it on the rack to dry. His body tenses and then relaxes when he sees that it is I, not my mother, who has entered the kitchen from the hallway. He frowns at me and turns back to his dishes.

"Why you got to do it?" Oldman continues, scratching the back of his gray head with one hand. In the other he holds his chopper.

"I the big man in my village," Thomas Scott tells Oldman, opening the refrigerator and taking out a carton of milk. "Egg," he says to me, without looking at my face. It is not a question.

"Okay."

"So you the big man," Oldman says. "You the big-big man, ehn?"

"Yeh, I the boss. I get electricity. I get money. Me part, I get respec' and got to carry it. I got to find one wife more." Thomas Scott takes a small glass bowl from the cabinet and places it on the counter next to the sink.

Before my father went away upcountry to oversee the lumbering of trees in the camps, I remember him telling me about Liberian customs. How it was common for men to marry twice or three times or more. A man with many wives is worthy of admiration, my father had said, because it meant that he had the means to support them. I stare at Thomas Scott, who is small, with evenly defined features. He rarely smiles and carries out his duties with an exacting calm, as if there is a method to pouring a glass of milk, a design to setting a table. Once I saw him catch a rat with his bare hands. It was running across the kitchen counter when his arm shot forward in a rush of speed. Then, over the kitchen sink, he had squeezed the rat's neck until a thin line of blood flowed from its ear, down his hand, and into the drain. His expression never changed. He may as well have been chopping an onion or drying a dish.

"So who goin' to be the next one?" Oldman inquires.

"I like Miatta," Thomas Scott replies, the way a person might say he likes white rice or peppermint gum.

Oldman laughs hard and long, his head tilted skyward toward the sun. "Miatta?" he hoots, slapping his knee with the blunt side of his cutlass. "That one workin' downtown Waterside? Ehn't you know she tie she face so? Every day she fini vex fo' something. Wha' you want marry that one fo'?"

Thomas Scott says nothing. With one hand he cracks two eggs, one after the other, into the bowl. He opens the utensil drawer, withdraws a fork, and begins beating the eggs with a clipped, even rhythm.

"Now, that one there workin' side Aba Jaoudi Market, that woman, Sarzah," Oldman continues, "she sweet like the sugar cane-o. Everybody got they eye on her." Oldman looks pensive for a moment. "But I ain' see her fo' long. You see her?"

Thomas Scott does not reply.

"Why you not ask her to be the second one, now?" Oldman asks, leaning into the door frame.

Thomas Scott opens the milk carton and pours an even flow of milk into the bowl. He resumes beating the eggs, but I notice his shoulders have stiffened into two angular points.

"I say, you not like Sarzah?"

"Sarzah was die last week." The words come fluidly, like the yellow egg that Thomas Scott pours into the frying pan. My pulse quickens in my veins.

Oldman is quiet. After a moment, he says, "Wha' you talkin', my friend?" His voice is so soft I can barely hear him.

"She die. Two day befo' yesterday. She get the

fever." Thomas Scott adjusts the flame beneath the pan. Oldman returns to his chair and fishes his pipe out of his bag. He strikes a match and for a long moment there is no sound but the uneven draw of tobacco smoke.

Thomas Scott empties the eggs onto a plate and sets a place for me at the kitchen table in the corner. "Eat," he says, and turns back to the dishes.

"What's the fever?" I ask.

"That nothin' to you. Eat you egg befo' it get cold."

Thomas Scott's shoulder blades are taut, held rigidly beneath his white shirt.

"I'm not hungry anymore," I say.

In three swift motions, Thomas Scott lifts my breakfast plate from the table, opens the screen door, and passes the food to Oldman. Oldman receives this offering in silence and begins eating. I leave my place at the table and stand in front of Oldman, quietly watching him eat my breakfast.

"What's the fever?" I ask. I feel hard but fragile on the outside, like the egg Thomas Scott cracked into the bowl. My insides are formless, swimming with anxiety and fear.

"Yellow fever." Oldman eats with solemnity. "You catch that one an' you die quick-quick."

"Why yellow?" My stomach pulls into itself, tight and hard.

"Whole body, whole face, change to yellow color," he says. A piece of egg tumbles from the fork onto his sweater. With his thumb and forefinger, he lifts the egg to his mouth and says, "That the genie-o. You do bad thing, genie comin' blow yellow something inside you ear. Then you color move to yellow an' you die."

I am mortified at this. Mortified, but also doubtful. "Who says?" I ask suspiciously.

"Everybody say that one. You not know nothin', small gal."

I try not to think about evil genies but the names of inoculations instead. I remember a few names of the injections I received before moving to Liberia—hepatitis, typhoid, gamma globulin—had I received a vaccination for yellow fever? Was there one? How did a person die from yellow fever anyway? And how could a fever be a color? I think about poor Sarzah, a woman I have never seen, beautiful but wilted, wasting slowly away as a sallow poison inks its way through her veins, leaking a yellow that stains her from the inside out. She would be lying in a yellow room, on yellow bed sheets, her skin turned a deathly pallor—

"I say, small gal," Oldman repeats, harkening me back to the wooden chair and the veranda. "Where the kola nut you bring me from Joe Ba'?"

"Some things are more important than a kola nut," I cry out, startling Oldman with my sudden outburst. I take a deep breath and look out into the yard, at the outstretched arms of the mango tree.

"Something jukin' that gal," Oldman says, scraping his fork on the plate.

Thomas Scott drops a glass in the kitchen. The shards skitter across the marble tiles.

The sun lifts itself higher above the yard as Oldman collects his things together, his whipper, his chopper, his pipe and matchbook, and places them into a plastic bag. He is going back to his village now, where he will push aside the daylight hours with quiet sleep until dusk falls again, when he will once more return to our yard.

"N'mind about the fever," he says, meaning that I shouldn't worry. He strolls away and calls over his shoulder, "Genie not get time fo' small-small Kwi Ma."

I stand on the veranda for a long time, feeling the tropical air thicken in the heat of late morning. I begin to worry about Boima. I wonder how I will hide him from the others.

"Why can't I have friends over?" I ask Te Te plainly, when I cannot think of a solution to my problem. She is dropping articles of clothing into the washing machine and does not answer right away because she is carefully measuring out soap powder. My mother has warned her that detergent is expensive. When Te Te finishes adding powder to the measuring scoop, she carefully taps the excess grains back into the box. She pours the soap into the churning water and swirls it around with her hand. The water grows darker and she frowns.

"Katrina Breslo come here one time," Te Te says.

"Katrina is little," I say flatly. "I mean someone my own age."

"Gal ain' get no own-age friend."

"I could make some," I say, carefully maneuvering my way around my sentences, as if each word were made of fragile glass. "I see lots of Liberian girls passing by the front gate. I could play with them." I wait to see how Te Te will respond.

"No African child comin' roun' here." Te Te shuts the washing machine lid. Hard.

"Why?"

"That what you ma say."

"Why?"

"That what she say. Not my business ask why. Why is fo' the yellow bird cryin' in the tree."

"You're just scared of my mother," I say bitterly. "Everybody around here is."

Sunlight reflects the anger in Te Te's eyes, and she places two wet hands upon my shoulders, shaking me roughly. "You mind wha' I say, now. Never bring no Liberian child to the house. Don't be makin' palava fo' everybody. Then you ma get vex with me, next you see I comin' loss my job." She shakes me again, harder this time, but I can see that she is shaking too. "You want me to loss my job?" she asks me, almost pleadingly. "That it you want? You fini make juju on me?"

I do not answer her. Instead I hold my place

42

inside her stare and think to myself, You may shake me, Te Te, but I will never crumble. I am stronger than that, and you will not keep me from finding a way to fill the hollow ache inside my heart. I am as slippery as the wind and as steadfast as the rock.

As if heeding my inner voice, Te Te releases me from her clutches and returns to the laundry. I stare unblinkingly at her back and resolve to find a way to bring Boima into the yard without telling anyone. I move away from Te Te and walk down the path leading to the swinging gate. I stretch my arms forward and curl my hands around the metal chain. Te Te's soapy fingers have left damp marks upon the sleeves of my dress, and it feels as if she were still holding on to my shoulders, still shaking me.

"I *will* find a way," I say loudly, into the air. The air does not answer me. But I know it can hear.

CHAPTER 6

Worn by Weakness

"Sarina?" my mother calls from inside the house. "Where are you?"

"I'm out here," I answer. I have been standing on the veranda for some time, and have not noticed the change in light resting on the leaves. A dull emptiness gnaws at my insides. It is lunchtime.

Inside the house, two places have been set in the dining room. From her place at the head of the table, my mother motions for me to sit beside her. She is wearing a light blue cotton dress and sandals. I study my mother carefully, watching for signs of low blood sugar. Thomas Scott watches her too, as he carefully places a large bowl of cut fruit upon the table. He returns to the kitchen briefly and emerges with a salad and a platter of sandwiches cut into triangles. I do not understand why Thomas Scott prepares so much food. My mother eats very little, picking at her meals like a sand crab.

"What shall we read today?" my mother asks me, lifting the napkin from her plate and unfolding it, square by square, onto her lap.

I shrug my shoulders. I do not enjoy this daily practice of reading.

"How about some Berryman?" my mother suggests. "Or Coleridge, Thomas Gray . . . Baudelaire," she runs through a long list of poets in her head. She knows so many of their works by heart, their words inscribed upon her memory from years of teaching and reading. I have never understood why she needs me to read at all.

"I think I'd like to hear the Irish today," she says suddenly. "Sarina, run and fetch me the collection by James Mangan."

I trudge down the long hallway to my parents' bedroom, where the walls are dark with wooden bookshelves. I run one finger along the smooth, uneven spines of volume after volume that my father packed into boxes before we moved to Liberia. When I locate *Mangan, James Clarence*, I yank it loose, return to the dining room, and lay it on the table beside my mother's plate.

"Here," I say.

"Read 'The Nameless One,'" she says, as if all she had to do was sift through the pages in her mind to choose the poem that suited her particular mood. I heave an exasperated sigh, skim through the table of contents, and find the poem.

*Tell thou the world, when my bones lie whitening
Amid the last homes of youth and eld,
That there was once one whose veins ran lightning
No eye beheld.*

*And tell how trampled, derided, hated,
And worn by weakness, disease, and wrong,
He fled for shelter to God, who mated
His soul with song—*

I stop reading and look hard at my mother, whose eyes are closed. These words are haunting, terrible, filled with a nightmarish vision. I cannot understand the meaning. Who is he that is *worn by weakness*? What does it mean to be *derided*? I don't want to read any more of this.

"Go on, Sarina, finish the poem," my mother says, folding her hands in her lap. She isn't seeing me. She isn't even hearing me. She listens only to the granite sound of words, each a solitary being that weaves its way into a mysterious pattern, separating me from my voice. I read quickly and without emotion, relieved when I reach the final stanza.

Tell how this Nameless, condemned for years long
To herd with demons from hell beneath,
Saw things that made him, with groans and tears, long
For even death.

At the last line of the poem, I slam the book shut. *With groans and tears, long for even death.* I shudder, not wanting to think about it. I lift a sandwich from the platter and begin eating.

"What do you think?" my mother asks me, reaching for the bowl of fruit.

"I hate it," I say. "It's stupid."

My mother sighs and takes a small bite of papaya. Thomas Scott stands by the kitchen door. Watching.

"Mom," I say, changing the subject. "Why did you tell Te Te that I'm not allowed to have friends in the yard?"

My mother does not answer. She stares thoughtfully at a square of fruit on the end of her fork.

"Mom, why?"

"Sarina, I just don't think it would be a good idea. I can't have you wandering around everywhere, not when I need you here with me—"

"But I wouldn't be wandering. I'd stay right in the yard. I'd bring my friends here."

"I'm sorry, Sarina, it's just not . . . it wouldn't be safe," she concludes, looking past me then, as if I were not really there at all, as if I were just a shadow to ponder between the cracks of light.

"Mom, please," I say. Something flares inside me, and I do not notice that my mother's sugar levels are falling, that her behavior is now becoming odd, exaggerated.

"No," she says. "No. No friends in the yard." She stands up and flies toward me, like a viper. Her fingers clamp my forearm.

"Let go of me, Mom," I say, because her grip hurts. She can be very strong when she is having a reaction.

"No," she says. "I will never let you go. Never."

"Mom, please, your sugar is low."

"No, it isn't," she insists angrily. She never knows when she is like this.

"It is, Mom, it is."

With my free hand I reach forward and grasp my mother's glass, still filled to the top with juice. My mother trembles in frustration, but will not let go of my arm.

"Mom, please drink the juice."

"No."

"You need it. Your sugar's low."

"It is not," she says again, raising her voice.

We go back and forth this way for a long time, my mother clutching my arm in painful desperation, me pleading with her to drink the juice that will restore her to her senses. But she refuses to listen, and turns her head from side to side so the juice spills across the white tablecloth.

Thomas Scott hurries back into the kitchen and returns with a full pitcher of juice. He pours another glass and places it on the table, next to my mother's plate. Her levels are dropping faster now, and she squeezes my arm tightly, as if she is trying to halt the flow of blood, as if she wants to squeeze the tears out from behind my eyes. But I will never let this happen. Not now, not ever. I wrench myself free of her, finally, and she collapses into the chair. I press the glass against her lips and hold it there until she swallows the juice, drop by drop. Thomas Scott silently pours a refill, and I force her to drink that too.

Gradually, her eyes grow clear. She sits up, slowly, and looks at me.

"You need to eat," I say, after a long silence. Like a child, she obliges, and picks up a sandwich between two pale fingers.

I sit slumped in the chair as I massage my throbbing arm, and watch my mother finish her meal. She is tired now, as she is so often after a reaction.

"I'm so sorry, Sarina," my mother says, now beginning to weep. "Can't you see how I need you?" She stands up, somewhat unsteadily, and Thomas Scott rushes to her side. He takes her arm and glares at me reproachfully, as if it were I who caused the entire episode.

"I'm just so tired," she says sadly. "Why am I so tired?"

"Goin' be all right," Thomas Scott says. His voice is smooth and unwavering and seems to calm her. He leads her down the hallway and toward the bedroom, where she will return to her cool sheets and float dreamlessly into sleep.

CHAPTER 7

If the River Doesn't Carry You, Carry Yourself

I am standing beneath the mango tree, wondering what to do about Boima. Where ·can we go where no one will find us, I wonder. I walk past the tree and around the side of the house, where grass and weeds curl around the edges, wild and unruly. Couldn't we lay low in the tall grass and hide? I almost laugh aloud at this idea, it seems so ridiculous. Besides, I am far too afraid of the crouching lizards and meandering snakes that hide between pointed blades of grass.

Farther around the house I study the banana tree. It is thin, with too few leaves to hide behind. Next I consider the tangled hibiscus hedge, the guava bush, and the red termite hill. But each has its own problem. The guava bush looks itchy and the hibiscus is too dark on the inside. And I do not even want to think about the termite hill, which is taller than I am and seething with insects. I hate ants, especially ones with giant heads and pinchers.

When I complete my tour around the house, I find myself beneath the mango tree once again. I stare at it with renewed interest. The branches look sturdy and comforting, concealed by an abundance of oval-shaped leaves. The way it holds the air and light is both solemn and magical, I think, and by the time I see Boima grinning at me through the holes in the front gate I have made my decision. We will hide in the mango tree.

When Boima slips past the gate I hold one finger to my lips and point with my other hand to the mango tree. He nods, and in a few graceful movements, lifts himself onto the lowest branch. I follow, though with considerably less grace. He grabs my wrist, and we climb upward toward slivers of sky that slip through cracks between the leaves. When we reach the tallest branch, I am startled at how high above the ground we have climbed. It is a little frightening.

"Don't lookin' down," Boima says.

"I'm not scared," I say. But Boima just smiles.

"Well, I'm not," I repeat, and we both laugh.

"You like plum?" Boima asks, pointing to a cluster of mangos hanging in between the leaves.

"You mean those mangos?" I ask.

"The Liberia people them, say 'plum,' " Boima explains.

"Oh. Well, no, I've never tried them," I admit.

"Never?" Boima's eyes open incredulously. "Whole tree you get an' you never try?" He reaches up and plucks a yellow-green mango, his eyes aglow with pride, as if he had invented the fruit himself. He takes a bite and hands it to me.

The mango is sour but not too bad. I take another bite and try not to make a face, which makes Boima laugh again.

"They not ready to go from they ma," he says. "Not fini grow up-o."

We eat them anyway. Boima's stomach swells with fruit, and I wonder if he has eaten anything else today.

"Sarina," Boima says, balancing a mango pit on the edge of a branch and looking at me intently. "Don't climb this tree by you one."

"Why not? I'm strong." I pull back my sleeve and flex a bicep to prove it. But Boima just stares at the gray streaks of finger-shaped bruises on my arm and looks into my eyes so questioningly, so sadly, that suddenly I am overwhelmed with the terrible feeling that I am going to cry. But this is no time for tears. I fight off the tightening circle inside my throat and say quickly, "So why can't I climb by myself?"

"To say why, I got to tell you one story," he says. "But my story too scary."

"I told you, I'm not scared of anything," I say, sitting up straighter on the tree bough.

"Ehn't you know one story 'bout snake in the plum tree?"

"You mean the *mango* tree," I tell him.

"The Liberia people them, say—"

"I know, I know. But we call it a mango tree, so I get confused when—"

Boima looks at me and smiles. He holds up one hand, palm outward, and asks again, "Ehn't you know one story 'bout snake in the *mango* tree?"

"No."

"Too scary-o."

"I'm listening."

"You comin' get so-so bad dream in the night."

"Try me," I say.

Boima settles back against the bark and closes his eyes halfway. He hitches his hands behind his head and says, "Once upon a time." Then he stops, waiting for something.

"Go on."

He sits up and opens his eyes. "You got to say 'time,'" he tells me.

"What?"

"That Liberian way. When somebody tell tale, you got to say 'time' after I say, 'Once upon a time.'"

"Oh."

"Once upon a time . . ." Boima begins again, leaning back.

"Time," I repeat.

". . . befo' the banana tree an' the eddo, befo' the Liberia people them was eat dumboy and fufu and so, there was grow one big-big mango tree. Mango tree was in one garden by she own self. Garden get the rubber tree an' the fern, but it not get nothin' to eat inside but the mango."

"Why?"

"Shh," Boima continues. "Hear me now. That

mango tree there, that the only one. An' everybody in the village want eat the sweet mango, but they too scary to do it."

"How come?" I ask.

" 'Cause everybody know that one bad-bad genie livin' inside the head o' the green mamba an'—"

"What's a green mamba?"

"That snake."

"Oh." A cold ripple runs along my back, despite the tropical heat.

"Yeh. So that genie snake, he jes' sit down, sit down, whole day in the mango tree. He eat the mango and the village people too scary to ask the snake fo' mango. But then one pekin, one small boy, he name Tuesday—"

"Tuesday?" I interrupt again. "What kind of a name is Tuesday?"

"Sarina, wha' you humbuggin' my story fo'? That boy name Tuesday 'cause he born on Tuesday."

"Oh, okay. Sorry."

"So that pekin Tuesday, he get kind heart, he a good pekin. But every day he got to listen the grumba grumba o' he hongry gut. He say to he village people, 'I comin' talk it with the snake,' but he ma say, he pa say, 'Ayah, my boy, don't do it-o. That snake will eat you.' But Tuesday say, 'Ma, Pa, if the river don't carry you, you got to carry you own self. Nobody bringin' food fo' the people, so I will get it my own way.' So he go to the mango tree and say, 'Oh, you snake, why you playin' sabi with my people, now? Ehn't you see we too hongry and want eat the mango?' Then Snake say, 'Woe be to you, small pekin. God hate me so and make me to crawl on my gut fo' shame. But one day, I find this tree and now I can smell the sky and see to the sun. I was get here befo' any y'all. So now this my tree an' you better move from here.'"

"So what happened?" I ask, fascinated.

"That boy, Tuesday, he a frisky boy-o. He get vex an' climb the tree to catch the mango. An' Snake get vex more and twist heself, juku juku, down from the tree an' fini bite that pekin head. An' the poison fillin' up that poor boy Tuesday an' he know he was comin' to die. But he jes' grab that snake by the neck and squeeze fo' long time. So when all the village people come now with they silver cutlass, they find one dead pekin and one dead snake. All two was die in the tree, jes' hangin' from the branch there. Now no way tho' two will ever see the sun again. An' Tuesday ma, she cry. An' Tuesday pa, he fini chop that snake head and bury it under the groun'."

"Why'd he do that?"

"Make the genie die."

"Oh. So what happened in the end?"

"That it."

"What do you mean, that's it?" I say. "What happened to the village?"

"Everybody eat mango from the tree."

"But that boy Tuesday, did he come back to life?"

Boima looks at me oddly. "When you die," he says solemnly, "you ain' never comin' back. Ehn't you know?"

"Yes, but how can that be the end of the story?"

"That the way."

"It's so sad," I say, shaking my head.

"Not sad."

"Why not?"

"That boy Tuesday, he do something good for he people. Now everybody free to eat the mango."

"I guess," I say, not entirely convinced.

"But remember this," Boima says, leaning forward and looking into my eyes. "Never climb the mango tree by you one. Snake who live in the mango tree never forget he brother. He vex every time. Keep all two you eye open."

I nod gravely at Boima. "Now tell me something happy," I say.

So Boima tells me about his wire baskets and the distinct rhythm of each color that he weaves into patterns. He says that every color has a spirit all its own, but that the shadowy greens and gritty yellows are his favorite, because they remind him of the sea. He talks about the orange spider on the web by his home and the smell of palm oil frying in his mother's pan. His words fall as evenly as light rain, and I am carried on the winds of stories that tumble from his tongue. Boima knows so many things.

Too soon, we notice that gray light is filtering down through the leaves of the mango tree. It is late. Boima lowers himself out of the tree and drops down on the grass below. And then he is gone, drifting away into the beyond, graceful as a sailing bird that merges with the horizon.

When I reach the ground, I find Te Te standing

on the veranda, staring into the front yard. How long has she been standing there, I wonder. Did she see Boima?

"Where you been, small gal?" she asks me.

"Nowhere," I say. "Just in the yard."

"Go inside," she says, though not unkindly. "Do you home study befo' you ma get vex with you."

"Okay," I say, relieved that she has not seen Boima. Te Te returns to the laundry room, but I linger for a moment on the veranda, remembering the afternoon. The sun weighs heavily upon the air, but now I think I can smell rain. Soon the branches of the mango tree will be burdened with heavy droplets that will run off the leaves, filling the holes in the ground with rainwater. I turn and run inside the house. I do not want to get wet.

Rash

I awaken to the darkness of my room. Except for the steady hum of the air conditioners, the house is silent, without motion or light. The insides of my ears are stinging and I want a drink of water. I reach over to my night table and switch on the lamp, which spills a path of yellow light across my room and into the hallway. I leave my bed and follow the light to the kitchen, where I know I will find one person who does not sleep amid all of this soundlessness.

"Oldman?" I call softly.

"Yeh."

It is comforting to hear his voice, even if I cannot see him through the slats of wood in the locked door.

"I'm getting a drink of water. I had a bad dream." It is not until I say these words that I realize that this is what had awakened me. Images of snakes twisting through holes in termite hills pass across my mind's screen, and I shudder.

"That the dream genie catch you-o," Oldman explains. He shifts his feet on the veranda tiles and it makes a smooth sound, like rushing water.

"Maybe." I pour myself a glass of cold water from a pitcher in the refrigerator. I notice that my lips are dry and cracked. The skin along my arms feels rough, as if I had been scratching in my sleep.

"Wha' you dream?" Oldman asks, probably glad for the company of another voice.

"Snakes," I say, taking another gulp of water. Under the dull light of the kitchen I notice a trail of strange red bumps along the length of my arms. The bumps are horribly itchy, but when I scratch them I am left with a burning sensation that feels even worse. I touch my fingertips to my eyelids, which are swollen. Again, the same fiery burn. I gasp.

"N'mind, yah," Oldman says, because he

thinks that I am reacting to the memory of my bad dream.

The kitchen door swings open. Beneath the dim light, clad only in his nightshirt, stands my father. He is small, like me, with blue eyes.

"Sarina, do you realize what time it is—" His voice catches in his breath suddenly, and he looks at me strangely. "What's happened to you?" He moves closer to me and stares at my face. I can feel his breath, warm and uneven, against my forehead.

"What is it?" I ask, frightened now, as my father examines my arms, at the spaces in between my fingers, where a redness runs along the skin like wildfire.

"It's a rash of some kind," he replies, turning my head from side to side with his thumb. "Have you been playing in the sand? Maybe you picked up a parasite from somewhere."

"I feel it on my legs too. It's hot."

My father cracks some ice cubes from a tray and drops them into a plastic bag. He ties the bag closed and wraps it in a dish towel.

"Hold this to your eyes," he says. "I don't think it's too serious, but tomorrow your mother will have to take you to the American Embassy.

There's a doctor there. He'll be able to tell exactly what this is—"

"Why can't you take me?"

"I'm going back to the bush very early in the morning, before you wake up."

"Again?" The word flings itself at my father like a little insect around a light bulb, and his cheek twitches.

"Sarina," my father says, focusing on something past me, something behind my head. The cabinet door, maybe. "Are you having trouble managing without me? Because you knew before we came here how important this work was to me, and how I need to count on you—"

"I know," I say quickly. "It's just . . . how will Mom take me to the embassy if you have the car?" I ask, holding the bag to my eyes. The ice cubes are cool, soothing.

"I'll have Thomas Scott go with the two of you. He can call a cab." He looks at me for a moment, but then quickly turns away, and heads for the kitchen door. He is going back to bed.

"Dad," I say, "wait."

"What is it?"

My father pauses and rests his fingers upon

the door handle. He stares at me blankly, and I want to tell him that things are not right, that since we moved to Africa the world has become stranger, that clocks tick in tropical seconds, that even the sun has a darkness and a warning and I do not think my mother likes it here.

"What is it, Sarina?"

"Nothing," I say. "A cab will be fine."

It is not until I am back in bed with the covers pulled up to the roots of my hair, the bag of ice pressed against my stinging eyelids, that I remember Oldman Jacob, sitting quietly outside the kitchen screen door, listening to the sound of the African night.

In the morning, the rash is worse. My tongue has swelled inside my mouth and one eye will not fully open. A blazing itch runs around the back of my neck and down my spine. I scratch it uselessly.

My mother holds a handkerchief to her mouth as she gets into the rickety yellow cab. She doesn't like to leave the house. She is afraid that she will catch some new germ that rides along African winds, something that will find its way into her body like the chigger and make her sicker than she already is. Thomas Scott sits in the front and talks quietly with the driver.

In the clinic at the American Embassy, I sit on a cold metal chair in the waiting room while my mother and Thomas Scott stand at the front desk. The nurse looks at them over her bifocals—first at my mother, then at Thomas Scott, then back to my mother again.

"This is a private clinic," she informs my mother. "We only treat Americans here." She taps a finger on the desk and stares.

My mother's voice is very low. "We're here for my daughter."

The nurse does not answer. But she points to a place on a piece of paper where my mother must sign. Thomas Scott hands her the pen, my mother signs, and they both sit down.

"Sarina?" The doctor opens the door to the examination room. He is short and wide, with dark hair. At the sound of his voice, all three of us stand up. The nurse quickly intervenes.

"I'm sorry," she says, not at all sounding like she is sorry. "But I can only allow family in with Sarina."

My mother nervously tucks a loose strand of

hair behind her ear. She is afraid that she will have a reaction here, and that I will be too busy with the doctor to help her.

"He's like family," my mother says, smiling weakly at the nurse.

"These are the rules," the nurse says. "Your"—she pauses, studying Thomas Scott over her glasses once more while she searches for the right word—"*help* will have to wait out here." Thomas Scott says nothing, and looks at the floor.

"How long have you been like this?" the doctor asks me once I am seated on the examination table, beneath fluorescent lights that hurt my eyes. Glass jars filled with cotton balls and tongue depressors line the metal counter.

"I woke up last night from it," I tell him, trying not to move my lips too much as I speak.

"Does it itch?"

"A lot."

"Burn?"

"Yes."

While the doctor asks me questions, I notice that my mother is not sitting in the chair that the doctor has set aside for her. Instead she hovers uneasily in the corner, like a butterfly with a broken wing. I can already see from here that her sugar is low. Not terribly low, but just enough that I can notice.

"Does she have any other allergies?" the doctor asks my mother as he gently touches the puffiness above one eye.

"No," I say.

"I see."

"How long have you been in Liberia?" he asks, this time turning around to look my mother in the face.

"Almost a year," I answer again.

"Your mother is a very quiet person," the doctor says. My mother makes a small noise, like something between a laugh and a whimper.

"Excuse me," I say, sliding off the examination table. I curse my mother silently, knowing that if she were not so nervous about leaving the house and coming to the American Embassy then her sugar levels would not have dropped. I open her purse and take out a piece of chocolate that she keeps for emergencies. I can feel the doctor's stare upon my back as I unwrap the candy and hand it to my mother. Miraculously, she eats it without further argument and sits down in the chair. I return to the examination table.

"Sorry," I say. I look into his eyes then, and see that they are brown, of the lightest hue. There is a softness to them.

"That's all right," he says.

"How did this happen?" he asks, gently touching the bruises on my arm.

"I fell," I say quickly.

"From what?"

"A tree." I look at my mother. The sugar has not yet taken full effect, and her eyes are gray and flat, like sky before rain.

"Was it a mango tree?" the doctor continues, opening a drawer and taking out a white prescription pad. He removes a pen from his chest pocket and begins to write something down. "Because you have just about the most severe case of mango rash that I have seen in quite some time. I'm prescribing triamicinolone, to be applied"—he pauses and looks over at my mother—"three times a day. Make sure you get it on her back," he says, staring at my mother for a long moment.

"I'll see to it," she says slowly, and tries to

smile. But I can see teardrops trembling inside her eyes.

Back in the waiting room, while the nurse stamps my paperwork and tells my mother where she can get the prescription filled, I run back to the examination room. The doctor is leaning over the metal counter, writing.

"Excuse me," I say. "But I just wanted to ask you. I—I really like climbing trees. Am I allergic to the mango tree?"

He laughs. "You can climb the tree all you like," he says. "But don't touch or eat the mango or you will surely break out into a rash again."

"Thank you," I say, letting out a big breath. I turn to go, but the doctor stops me.

"Sarina?"

"What?"

"How long has your mother been a diabetic?"

His question hits me like a jolt of electricity.

"How did you know?" I ask.

"Doctors know these things."

"Since she was a child," I say, and shrug my shoulders.

"Has it always been this . . . erratic?" he asks. His kind eyes search my face for reasons, explanations.

"I guess. She can't help it. It's always been hard for her to control her sugar levels." I do not tell him that since we moved to Africa my mother has stopped seeing me, and that her reactions make her act differently now. Meaner.

"And where is your father?"

"At work a lot," I admit. "But Thomas Scott is here all the time."

"Is that the gentleman in the waiting room?"

I nod. "And Te Te. She helps too." The doctor's expression makes me feel uncomfortable so after a brief pause, I add, "And Oldman Jacob."

"Still," he persists. "It seems like a lot for a twelve-year-old to take on."

I shrug again. "I can manage."

The doctor smiles. "Of course," he says, but when he glances at the chart lying on the counter I think I hear him say, "We'll see."

My mother pokes her head into the examination room then, and laughs nervously when she sees the doctor. "I was looking for you, Sarina," she says.

"We were just having a little chat," the doctor says pleasantly, stepping away from the counter and laying a hand on my shoulder. "I wanted to make sure Sarina understood how to apply her medication. But it seems to me that she already knows exactly what to do. You're lucky to have such a responsible daughter."

"That I am," my mother says, holding the door open for me. I glance at the doctor before walking out, and he winks.

It begins to rain on the drive home. Through the slow drizzle of raindrops I look out at the road. The taxi rushes by women sitting on low stools under tall umbrellas, selling oranges and grapefruit from chipped enamel bowls. Boys sell candy from small wooden tables and I wonder how long they will sit in the rain in hopes of earning a few coins. I hold a tube of mango rash medication in my hand and watch two clear drops of rain touch and unite on the window-pane. I wonder what Boima is doing today. I hope he will visit me again soon.

CHAPTER 9

Pepper Soup

Two jars of boney fish are missing from the kitchen pantry. Thomas Scott has counted them twice. We have no electricity and the air is still and quiet without the air conditioning, so I can clearly hear my father on the telephone down the hall, using words I do not understand, like "philistine" and "corruption." But my mother's voice is much higher, and louder, too, because she is furious. The dried fish Te Te buys from the market, which Thomas Scott keeps in tightly sealed glass jars because my mother swears she can detect an odor even through the plastic bags, are absolutely nowhere to be found.

"No," she shouts from the kitchen. "Count them again, Thomas Scott. Count them again."

"Missy, I count it. My hand to God, I count it."

But he does check again. I can hear him from the dining-room table, where I am trying to do my lessons. Each time he counts, the number comes up the same, two jars short. My mother is fuming, and tosses things from the pantry shelves onto the floor in a terrible rage. Even without the diabetes, she has always had a very bad temper.

I cannot concentrate on my studies amid all of this noise, so I push open the front door and step outside. The air is just as warm on the veranda, but it feels purer, less stale than indoors. Te Te is chatting with Flomo by the front gate. He is chewing on his familiar toothpick and eating a mango at the same time. Te Te laughs and slaps her thighs when she talks to Flomo, but when she sees me coming down the path the smile disappears from her face like a necklace down a sink drain.

"Hey, small gal," Flomo says.

"Hi."

"Wha' news?"

"We lost our electricity," I tell him.

"That the way," Flomo says. He is right. That is the way in Liberia.

"Why you not doin' study?" Te Te asks me. She sniffs and straightens out the invisible wrinkles in her dress.

"I can't think. Dad's yelling something into the telephone and Mom is shouting at Thomas Scott because two jars of boney fish are missing."

Suddenly Te Te mentions something about ironing and work, and hurries away.

"What are you doing here, anyway?" I ask Flomo, after Te Te has gone.

"I on my way to Breslo people there. To garden."

"Flomo," I plead. "Can't you take me with you? I want to see Katrina's monkey."

"Well . . ." Flomo takes one last bite from his dripping mango and tosses the pit into a nearby cluster of ferns. The leaves make a noise, as if ruffled by the invasion.

"Please?"

"Where my blue-eye smile?" Flomo teases. I stretch my lips as wide as they will go and hope that even my posterior teeth are showing. Flomo laughs and says again, "That the way."

During the five-minute walk to Katrina's house, I worry for a moment about my mother.

She will be angry if she finds that I have left the yard. Quickly, I pound this thought down, the way the Liberians mash the cassava root with mortar and pestle. Maybe today will be one of those days that she does not notice.

The Breslos live down the dirt path, just past an old soccer field. Katrina is their only daughter, and I do not care for her much.

"Well, hello, Sarina," Mrs. Breslo calls from inside the kitchen. She wipes her hands on a yellow dish towel and waves to me. I run up the steps and find Katrina standing behind her mother, her fat hands and dimpled cheeks smeared with chocolate frosting.

"What happened to your face?" Mrs. Breslo asks, looking at me with surprise and concern. For a moment I am bewildered, but then I remember. Mango rash. Although I have not been itchy for a few days, there is still a hint of redness snaking across my eyelids and down one side of my cheek.

"Wha' I mus' do today, missy?" Flomo asks Mrs. Breslo.

"The front hedges, please, Flomo," she tells him. "And cut it all down. It grows back so quickly in this rain."

"Mango rash," I tell Mrs. Breslo.

"Want to see my monkey?" Katrina asks. Her eyes are small and hard, like blue rocks.

"Mango what?" Mrs. Breslo looks confused.

"It doesn't itch anymore," I tell her. "The American Embassy gave me cream."

"Come on," Katrina whines. "Let's go see the monkey."

Mrs. Breslo wipes Katrina's face with the corner of her apron. "Don't tease the poor thing," she says, and turns back to her mixing bowl.

Outside I can hear the *swish ching* of the hibiscus bush being cut down, and the quiet fall of twigs on soft grass. Katrina's monkey is locked inside a square bamboo cage that barely contains room enough for it to stand. It makes a noise when it sees us, a mournful cry that fills me with an ache and sorrow.

"What do you call him?" I ask her, after she has unlocked the cage and I am holding the tiny monkey to my chest. It is not much larger than my hand.

"Ticky," Katrina says. "Listen to the sound he makes. It's like a clock."

Ticky makes a clicking noise as he climbs carefully down the front of my dress and searches my pockets for something to eat. He is delicate and slow-moving, without the agility one would normally expect from a monkey.

"What's wrong with him?" I ask.

"He lost a piece of his tail when he got shot down, see?" Katrina grabs the end of the monkey's tail and points to a bloody red scab. Ticky lets out a piercing screech while Katrina, unaffected by the noise, tells me, "My mother says he doesn't have any balance now."

"Katrina, let go, you're hurting him."

"He's my monkey," she says defiantly, lifting the animal from my arms. Ticky leans forward and licks the frosting on Katrina's chin.

"Eeeuuw," she cries, batting Ticky away from her. The monkey screams again and falls to the ground. He cowers by his cage, crying pitifully.

"You shouldn't be so rough with him," I tell her, feeling a little sick.

"Most of the time he just stays in his cage," Katrina shrugs, and her blond curls bounce against her shoulders.

I do not say anything. My heart feels as if it is being wrung from its rib cage.

"Let's play something," Katrina decides autocratically.

"All right."

"Put Ticky back in the cage," she commands.

"Can't he stay out?"

"No."

I cannot believe that I am being made to carry out the demands of a spoiled six-year-old child. So I decide to outsmart her instead.

"Katrina."

"What?" She squashes a small bug beneath her white sneaker.

"I have a good idea for playing house. Want to hear?"

"Yeah, okay."

"I'm the big sister and you're the little sister, and—"

"I don't want to be the little sister. Why do I always have to be little?"

"Fine, you can be the big sister too."

"How can there be two big sisters?" she argues.

I take a deep breath, almost wishing that I had stayed home.

"Okay," I say. "I'll be the little sister. And Ticky will be the little *baby* sister."

"How can a stupid monkey be a baby?"

"We can pretend that the father is away at

work, and the mother is in bed, dying of a terrible sickness."

"What kind of sickness?"

"Of . . . poison. She has just been bitten by a deadly snake."

"How?" Katrina wants to know.

"Well . . ." I struggle for a moment, jogging my brain for ideas. "While their mother was in the shower, an evil snake, the most venomous serpent that lives in Africa, the green mamba, slithers up from under the drain and bites her on the ankle. Right away, the poison flows into her veins, and she becomes very sick."

"That can't happen," Katrina says, her eyes widening. "Shower drain holes are too small."

"Believe me, it happened," I assure her. "And now the mother is going to die and we have to take care of the baby."

"Here, we can put this on him," Katrina says excitedly, pulling a towel from the clothesline and wrapping it around the monkey. Immediately, it screams again.

"Be gentle, Katrina."

"It's *my* monkey," she repeats, grabbing Ticky by the leg as he wriggles his way out of the towel.

As the hour passes, I manage to convince Katrina that the baby must be treated gingerly, with love and extra attention, because its mother is too sick to care for it. By the time the last pile of shorn leaves and broken twigs has been cleared away beneath the Breslo's kitchen window, and Flomo has collected his gardening tools, Katrina is cradling Ticky in her arms and whispering, "Don't worry, baby, your two big sisters will take care of you after Mama is gone."

"Bye, Katrina," I call, longing to take the monkey home with me, to hold it in my own warm embrace.

Katrina snaps to attention, and the monkey tumbles to the ground once more. "I didn't say you could leave," she hollers. "I didn't say!"

Mrs. Breslo waves an apologetic good-bye while Katrina shrieks and beats a wooden spoon against the kitchen counter.

"Flomo," I say as we walk along the path. "Is that monkey locked up every time you come to garden?"

"Yeh."

"That cage is too small," I tell him. "It's cruel." We walk in silence for a few moments.

"Small gal," Flomo says, his eyes dancing in

the sunlight. "You know wha' I comin' do when I get my own of monkey?"

"What?" I ask listlessly, kicking up little dust circles on the road with my sandals.

"I goin' drop that monkey in the pot," he says, and breaks up laughing.

"You would not," I say, offended that he would even say such a thing. How could someone like Flomo, as free-spirited as a gust of wind, do something so premeditated, so cold and unfeeling?

"I comin' do it," Flomo says, nearly collapsing on the path with laughter. "I comin' make my pepper soup!"

I open the gate to my yard and pretend not to hear him.

"Pepper soup," he whoops as he ambles away, back to wherever it was that he came from.

"It is not funny," I call, heading toward the kitchen, where I can hear Thomas Scott and Te Te arguing over how to make a fruit salad. I do not look back.

CHAPTER 10

Flowers That Open
and Grass That Grows

"**A**nd then he said he would eat a monkey. Can you believe that?"

We are hiding in the mango tree, and I am telling Boima about Ticky and Flomo's dreams of making pepper soup. I am excited to see Boima after so many days. He has been busy at the marketplace, selling his baskets. He has also begun to sell fruit for his ma.

"Boima," I say, because an important question presses upon me. "Would you ever eat a monkey?"

"Sometime," he admits, and looks away.

"Oh." I am sad to learn this.

"Sarina," Boima says, "white people an' African people, they different. African boy eat the palm nut an' the country chop. He like hot mala pepper. He chew boney. Hongry time comin', boy got to eat wha' he can get."

I look at Boima, at his thin legs hanging over the branch of the mango tree. The bones in his wrists and elbows jut out at awkward angles, and his clothes hang loosely on his body. A breeze could lift and carry him away.

"Well, I'm never going back to Katrina's again," I tell him. The memory of Katrina hurling the baby monkey to the ground passes through me like a breath of hot wind. How could anyone be so cruel?

Boima nods, as if he has heard my thoughts. "Man got to respec' the animal in the bush," he says solemnly. "Got to love the fish like the fish love water." We reflect on this for a moment.

"I would love to teach Katrina a lesson."

"Yeh," Boima agrees.

"Boima, tell me a story," I beg him. "Please."

Boima's eyes glow like bright embers, and he lowers his voice. "I know one story 'bout juju," he says.

"Juju," I whisper, because the words sound ominous, as if they might conjure up the spirits.

"That magic something," Boima explains, settling back onto the branch and readying himself for another story. "Once upon a time . . ."

"Time," I repeat.

"There was one man who get two wife. First wife name Kulana, an' she sweet pass all. She get face that make the flower open an' grass want grow. But second wife, name Sietta, she the ugly cloud that open to gray rain an' kill the flower."

"Why'd he marry her then?"

"Shh. Grown man get funny way sometime."

"Oh."

"So Sietta heart too cold, an' every day she pray to God that first wife will get mix up in devil business. Then one day, Kulana make a fine palm butter to eat with rice an' boney. Everybody in the village want kiss Kulana hand that beat the greens to go inside the sauce. Everybody 'cept fo' Sietta. Sietta heart was grow dry when she smell Kulana sauce boilin' choogoo choogoo in the pot. So she decide to spoil it. She fini drop plenty hot pepper inside Kulana own an' make one different palm butter she own way."

"She ruined Kulana's palm butter?"

"Dry heart can do all kind a something to

people," Boima remarks. "So Kulana give to the people the palm butter an' everybody jes' chokin', all they eye gone red. An' Sietta say, 'Oh, my people, ehn't you want try my own tasty palm butter here?' So the people try it and like it too much so second wife grow big pass Kulana."

"Wasn't Kulana mad?" I ask.

"Yeh. She know Sietta fini mean her. But Kulana blood runnin' sweet like sugar, an' she want good-good thing fo' everybody. So she ask the genie to make good juju on Sietta, to change the ugly cloud that open to gray rain that kill the flower."

"So what did the genie say?"

"Genie say, 'Kulana, go climb the coconut tree and shake down two coconut, one fresh an' sweet, the other dry like bone. Then dig two hole in the ground, side by side. Next crack the dry coconut an' drop it in one hole. Then take the sweet juice and fini pour it inside the other one.'"

"Why?"

Boima ties his face at me and says, "Sarina, why you hurry-hurry me?"

"Sorry."

"So the genie say to Kulana, 'Drop on you knee an' open the two hole together to make one big-big space in the ground. Let the sweet coconut juice flow into the dry.' "

Boima leans forward, swinging his thin legs in anticipation of the ending.

"An' so, Kulana do like the genie say an' sweet connec' to dry. An' all goin' roun' an' roun' inside one open circle in the earth. An' Kulana love carry to Sietta. Next day, Sietta heart change from sour plum to sweet-sweet yam, an' she forget to hate. Now Sietta get the face that make the flower open and grass want grow."

Boima says the final lines of his story with great dramatic flourish and beams proudly at me.

"So all she had to do was spill some coconut juice and Sietta was changed forever?" I ask dubiously.

"That juju too strong," Boima says knowingly.

Suddenly I am struck with an idea.

"Boima?"

"Yeh."

"Do you think *we* could make juju?"

"Wha' you talkin?"

"I mean, couldn't we use it to change Katrina?" I half expect Boima to laugh at my suggestion, but he only looks at me, his round eyes wide open, listening.

"We can try it-o," he says.

So we do. There are no coconut trees nearby, but Boima says what kind of fruit we use does not matter so much.

"You ready?" Boima asks, after we have slid down the mango tree and made two small impressions in the earth with our fingers. For the dry we select an old guava, and for the sweet we both decide an orange would be best. But I have to run into the house to find one, because there are no orange trees in the yard.

"So this guava is Katrina," I say, after I have returned moments later. Boima nods and takes the orange from my hands. He squeezes the juice into the second hole and then leans back on his heels.

"An' the orange?" Boima asks.

I think this over for a moment and decide that there is only one answer to this question.

"The sweet orange is you," I say, feeling a little bit embarrassed.

"I?" Boima responds, surprised.

"Yes," I say. Something loosens deep inside me, as clear and warm as light. "You are the sweetest person I know." I have to push the words out.

Boima presses his knees into the damp ground below the mango tree. As we burrow the tunnel that joins the two circles together, I realize suddenly that we are doing more than simply digging a hole in the dirt. We are taking part in something magical, something bigger than us, and we are best friends. The air has a presence all its own and neither of us speaks, not wanting to fill the space with the emptiness of words.

And then the quiet is attacked by the sound of glass exploding on marble tiles. My heart pounds to a faster rhythm. My mother.

"Wait here," I tell Boima, and race toward the house.

In the kitchen my mother has dropped a blue porcelain bowl. Jagged pieces scatter across the white tiles, like bits of sky through clouds. A pound bag of sugar, half open, has fallen from the counter and spilled across the floor. There is a numbness to my mother's movement as she holds on to the counter, trying to stand upright. Her sugar is low.

"Three jars missing," she says, dropping to the floor and attempting to pick up the pieces of broken glass. "Did you count them, Thomas Scott?"

"Six time, missy," he says. "Three jars gone fo' true."

"Oh, Thomas Scott." She begins to cry then, and leans against him as he kneels beside her on the kitchen floor. "Who is stealing from us?"

"I don't know-o," he says softly. "I don't know."

I watch them on the kitchen floor for a long moment. My mother's body has gone limp like the half-spilled bag of sugar, leaving her empty and white, without spirit.

I back away, because I will have to help my mother, and I must tell Boima to leave. When I reach the mango tree, I am horrified to find Te Te standing next to the trunk, looking up into the leaves like a hunting dog that has just treed a raccoon or a fox.

"Te Te," I say, feeling like I am about to be sick. Am I too late?

But Te Te looks startled, as if I had caught her in a secret act. She looks at me with an odd expression that I cannot interpret, and hurries away.

"Boima?" I whisper, after Te Te has gone.

"Yeh."

"You have to go. My mother is sick," I tell him. Boima nods and climbs down from the tree. I watch him go and then rush back to the house. Thomas Scott meets me just outside the screen door. There is a trace of sugar stuck to his right cheek, and he looks off-balance, frightened.

"Sarina," he says, his voice shaking. "Go to the phone. Call you pa upcountry. You ma"—he pauses, and takes a breath—"she not all right."

I nod obediently and run into the house.

CHAPTER 11

Genie in the Water

"Be good, Sarina," my father says as he gets into the car. "Don't leave the yard without Te Te. Oldman Jacob will mind you at night. We'll be back in a week." They are going to a health resort in Ghana, many hours away. There my mother will get the rest she needs, without distractions.

"Your mother is not doing very well," my father had said to me earlier as he packed three dresses, a nightgown, and a pair of sandals into my mother's travel bag. I did not tell him that I knew this already, that it had taken her a very long time to regain consciousness after I had fed her spoonfuls of sugar dissolved in water. That I had been scared.

"She can't help the way she is," my father told me. "You do understand that, don't you?"

I had nodded, because I wanted my father to think that yes, I did understand that diabetes can do strange and terrible things to people. But truthfully I have never been sure where my mother leaves off and the diabetes begins. Does the disease make her angry and afraid all the time, even when she is not having reactions?

I wave good-bye until red dust rises behind the spin of the car tires and my parents are gone. Then I sigh, and wonder if Boima will visit today.

"Small gal, you better go inside an' do you school study," Te Te says from behind me. Now that my parents have left, I consider telling Te Te about Boima. The secret aching place that holds my tears inside longs to hear Te Te tell me that it would be fine to walk along the city streets with Boima, or to celebrate the sparkling blueness of the sea. But I know this is just a daydream. Te Te will never disobey my parents' orders and allow me to leave the yard. She does not want to risk losing her job.

I walk into the dining room, where my textbooks are stacked on the table. It is cold in here, and I notice that Te Te has left her sweater hanging neatly over the back of a chair. It is blue and soft, and smells like a bar of soap. I hold the sweater to my cheek for a moment and wonder how a person who chooses to wear such softness could be so harsh, so rigid and unfeeling. As I lay the sweater back over the chair, I notice something heavy inside the left-hand pocket. Curious, I reach in and take out a small glass jar. I hold it in my hand, not believing for a moment what I have found. Boney fish. A tightly sealed glass jar of boney fish.

Te Te opens the door then, and finds me standing by the dining-room chair, the jar of boney fish in my hand. The air pulses with recognition, and we stare at each other.

"You stole the boney fish?" I ask in disbelief. "Why?"

Te Te does not answer me. Except for the eyes, her features are fixed and smooth, like faded carvings on old stone. But I catch a flickering light inside her eyes as speedily as the net traps the buzzing fly. Te Te is afraid.

"I should tell my mother," I begin, weighing the jar thoughtfully in my hand. A rush of something cold and powerful passes over me, as if I am standing behind a waterfall. I hold the jar of boney fish and observe Te Te's expression for one more moment before pushing open the front door and walking out to the veranda. I need to think about how I will make use of my recent discovery. Surely it would be unfair to use the boney fish to blackmail Te Te. But why not? What has Te Te ever done for me? I think for a long while, until I hear the tinny sounds of silverware being placed upon the dining-room table by Thomas Scott, until Boima is waving at me from behind the front gate. Until I have made up my mind.

"I want you to meet someone," I tell Boima, leading him up the path to the veranda, where Te Te is slicing an apple into a purple bowl.

But Boima doesn't want to show himself, and fidgets while I make the introductions. Te Te does not smile. Boima looks at his toes.

"Boima," I say, looking directly into Te Te's face. "Can you take me to the ocean today?"

Boima mumbles something like yeh, he thinks he can do that one there.

"Good."

I lean toward Te Te and hope that my stare

weighs heavily upon her spirit. "Now we both have secrets to keep," I whisper. A shadow the color of sadness passes behind Te Te's eyes, and I wonder if I have made a bad decision. But then Boima and I are hurrying to the sea and thoughts of Te Te are swept clean away, like sand beneath the wave at the water's edge.

The ocean is wider than I had imagined. It is coal gray, the color of stones, the color of sky before rain. I break into a run across the sand, fast and furious, and do not stop until I have reached the water. I look back and Boima is far behind, a tiny melting dot on a warm stretch of yellow sand.

"Sarina, come back, yah," he calls, but I do not listen. I run into the water still wearing my dress, and the ocean spirals a powerful current around my legs. Towering waves block the horizon, catching a hint of sunlight before washing over me, cooling a heat inside my body that I did not even know was there.

"It's like magic," I call to him as a wave knocks me sideways, soaking me through. "Why don't you come in?"

But Boima will not come any closer than the

water's edge. He paces back and forth on the sand and yells something that I cannot hear over the noise of the waves.

"What?" I shout.

" . . . in the water, genie in the water," he cries in alarm.

Genie in the water? What is he talking about, I wonder. I squint at the torrid rush of waves that gather strength from beneath the surface, pulling me inward as they hurl themselves toward the beach. I dig my heels into the wet sand but cannot avoid the pull into deep water that rises quickly to my chest. I am a little frightened now, and understand what Boima meant by a genie in the water. He is talking about the undertow.

A giant wave, glorious but terrible, charges along the water's surface and curls above me, like a scorpion's tail. When it collapses, the salty foam burns through my nostrils and throws me above and below the tide, as helpless as a flopping fish inside a bear's paw. I am stunned by the sheer force of the waves, and struggle to find my way back to the sand, where Boima is hopping on his skinny legs like a nervous egret.

"It's a little rough out there," I tell him, after I have cleared my throat of saltwater. Boima does not answer me. He is probably wondering why the genie did not decide to eat me that day.

"There's no such thing as genies," I try to explain to him, as we make the trek across the sand to the other side, where the lagoon stretches peacefully behind some palm trees. "It's just an undertow."

But Boima does not even look at me until we are both immersed in the still water of the lagoon, where it is safe, where there are no waves or genies. Beneath the water we join hands and open our eyes inside the quiet fluid of an inner world tinted green, where movement is beautiful because it is so simple.

We swim all afternoon, until the shadows under the palm trees extend beyond the point where the lagoon water meets the sand, where a crowd of Liberian children and teenagers has gathered. They are shouting and frantically waving their arms at us.

"Boima," I say, noticing suddenly that we are all alone. "What are they staring at?"

Boima looks behind us, and we see something

that makes us both gasp. A snake. It is shiny and black, and loops across the water in graceful pursuit of the shore, moving in our direction.

"Swim," I scream at Boima, and dive under, never letting cease the flow of movement until my fingers touch the wet sand at the water's edge. But Boima does not move. He treads water in the middle of the lagoon, his head swiveling back and forth between the approaching snake and the sand.

"Move from there," the Liberians call, but Boima is paralyzed with fear and may as well be trapped inside a frozen circle of ice. I cannot bear to think of what could happen if the snake finds Boima blocking its journey to the shore, so I decide to go back into the water and get him. When I wade into the lagoon once more, the children cry out at me to stop it—what are you doing you small gal you crazy get out from the water ehn't you know snake coming bite you—but I don't have a choice. I run into the water and dive toward Boima. When I reach him, there is a wild glaze in his eyes and his face has emptied of color.

"Kick your legs," I tell him as I grab his thin arm.

"I can't make it," he whispers. "Snake comin' catch me-o."

A curvy line trails behind the snake as it skims sideways along the surface of the water, and I know we don't have much time.

"You have to make it," I tell him, because I do not want to think about what will happen if he doesn't. I hold on to Boima's wrist and sweep the water with my free arm, long and wide like a boat's oar, to drive myself forward. My feet make desperate, panicky splashes and I know that we are not moving very quickly. The snake winds along the water right behind us, and I swim harder, because now when I look back I am close enough to catch a glimpse of its tiny eyes, so hard and black, and the pink flickering of its forked tongue. I kick and pull and splash while the children cry out at us to hurry, but I am just too tired suddenly, and am about to tell Boima that I am very sorry, that I do not think I can swim another inch, when I feel the grainy sands beneath my feet and we have reached the edge.

The black snake is a cobra. It rises proudly above the sand and flattens its neck muscles, poised and ready to strike. But too many people surround the snake, beating it with sticks and rocks, and it does not have a way to protect itself. Then a teenage boy raises a cutlass high above his head and makes a sideways slice into the air. The blade connects, and the pointed head flies upward, almost swaying in the wind before falling to the ground.

"It's dead," I whisper to Boima, who has kept his eyes closed the entire time.

"They bury the head?" he asks.

"They're doing it now," I tell him as two boys push the severed head into a hole with long sticks. They cover it with sand.

"Boima?"

"Yeh." Boima's eyes are still closed. He presses his face into the ground. Sand cakes his cheek.

"I guess lagoons have genies too."

Boima does not respond to this. He is either sleeping or ignoring me, I cannot tell which.

I do not think we will be returning to the ocean again very soon.

CHAPTER 12

Rogues

I sit up straight in bed. I have just heard an odd noise, a cry of some kind, long and low. I flick the switch on my table lamp but nothing happens. Blackness. The house is silent and the air conditioners are not humming. We have lost our electricity.

I leave my bed and feel my way around the end table and the dresser until I reach the doorway to the hall. I hate this feeling of unseeing, of blackness and silence, and as I trail my hands along the walls of the dark hallway, I wish things were different. I wish my parents were here. I wish I were not alone in this house. I wish I did not live in Africa.

When I reach the kitchen door I hear it again.

The cry. It is haunting and plaintive, like someone or something in pain. I open the kitchen door and face a darkness so empty and still that I cannot help but wonder if this is what it is like to be unconscious.

"Oldman?" I say. No answer. My blood pulses violently in my ears.

"Oldman, are you there?" I call again. Nothing. I move my hands from the top of the old stove to the counter, running my fingers along the surface until I feel the metal spout of the water filters. Below the filters there is a drawer, which makes a noisy clattering sound as I pull it open and fumble around for a flashlight. I try not to think about my fingertips grazing the backs of large cockroaches that sometimes nest in utensil drawers. When I find the flashlight, I switch it on and a long beam spotlights the wooden slats in the door leading outside.

"Oldman," I say, unlocking the door and stepping onto the veranda. I shine the light on his wooden chair. It is empty. I wave the flashlight back and forth around the yard, but it only gives me a keyhole view of the outdoors, a patch of grass, a section of mango tree, four bricks in the wall of the house.

"Where are you?" I cry out, my throat tightening.

Then I hear it. A low moan from somewhere in the back of the yard, past the lean banana tree, beyond the hibiscus hedge. I take a few steps into the backyard. "Is that you, Oldman?" I call.

"Here me."

"Where?" I shine the flashlight everywhere, under the low-growing papaya tree, inside a cluster of green leaves, on the termite hill. The slim ray of light from the flashlight is not wide enough to cut through the infinite darkness of the yard, not bright enough to find Oldman.

"This way." I take a few tentative steps into the grass, praying that all the tropical creatures, the serpent and the spider, have gathered that an intruder with a light is interrupting their sleep, and are looking elsewhere to hide.

"Which way?"

"Here. By the tree."

He is lying on the ground, beneath the almond tree in the backyard.

"What happened?" I ask, shining the light on his face. A thin river of dark red blood flows from a wide cut on his forehead. The blood drips onto a smattering of crushed almonds by his ear, collecting in a little pool of red and green.

"That rogues fini juke me."

"Rogues?"

"Yeh. Two of them. They cut the fence."

I turn the flashlight to the wire fence, fifty feet away. A semicircle of wire has been cut open, big enough for a body to push its way through. My stomach grows cold. "Are they still here?" I whisper.

"No. I run behind them. They throw stones to my head. One big-big stone catch me, but I jes' hold up my whipper an' they run." Oldman speaks very slowly, as if he is about to fall asleep.

"Well, you can't just lie here. You're bleeding." I take his arm and try to pull him upright, but he is as heavy and lifeless as a bag of sand.

"Come on," I urge. "Get up."

"Sarina, I not able it, I too dizzy-o. I leavin' small to die."

"No! I won't let you die." The blood still flows from Oldman's wound, and I think back to years ago, when my mother sliced her hand on a tin can during a bad reaction. She had pressed a folded dish towel against the cut to slow the stream of blood.

Quickly, I pull off one of Oldman's boots and then his sock, which I fold over twice and hold against his forehead. "Keep that there," I tell him, lifting his hand to his face.

Oldman is quiet. He closes his eyes.

"Don't sleep," I say, terrified that he will die there, under the tree, in a mix of blood and almonds. "I'm going for help."

"Yeh."

I run back into the house, down the hall and into my parents' bedroom, where there is a telephone. I throw open the door and search through the papers inside my father's night-table drawer until I find a small book with telephone numbers in it. I flip to the *B*s and dial the Breslo family. The phone rings twice, and a man's voice, hoarse from sleep, answers the phone.

"Hello?"

"Mr. Breslo?"

"Who is this?"

"It's Sarina. From down the road."

"Oh, Sarina." His voice changes. "Is something wrong?"

"Yes. My parents are in Ghana and our night watchman is hurt."

"What?"

"Rogues threw rocks. He's bleeding and almost"—I cannot bear to say the next word and so say—"asleep."

"Oh my God. Where is he now?"

"Under the almond tree." I struggle to keep my tears at bay.

"We'll be right there."

"Wait."

"What is it?"

"We have no electricity."

"I'll bring a flashlight."

Ten minutes later I run down the path and unlock the front gate. Both Mr. and Mrs. Breslo are in the car and Katrina is in the back seat, asleep, her blond head leaning against the car window.

"Where is he?" Mr. Breslo asks. He is bald except for a silver fringe of hair around the back of his head. His stomach protrudes beneath a white T-shirt.

"This way," I say, leading him into the backyard. Mr. Breslo kneels by Oldman and removes the sock from his forehead. Oldman is silent.

"Is he . . . dead?" I ask, nearly choking on the air.

"No. He's unconscious. It looks like he's lost

a fair amount of blood. We're going to have to take him somewhere, for stitches."

"I get my whipper and my chopper," Oldman mumbles.

"What did he say?" Mr. Breslo asks me.

"His weapons," I tell him.

"Well, at least he's talking. Help me lift him up, Sarina. Then I'll drive him to Cooper Clinic." Cooper Clinic is a missionary hospital about five miles away.

Mrs. Breslo opens the passenger-side door, her face pale with concern, as we approach the car. Oldman leans heavily against Mr. Breslo, who grunts beneath the extra weight.

"Oh my God," she says, when she sees the spatterings of blood on Mr. Breslo's white undershirt and my nightgown. "Oh dear God," she keeps repeating.

Mrs. Breslo lays Katrina down on the sofa in our living room while we wait for Mr. Breslo to return from Cooper Clinic. "What's happening?" Katrina asks drowsily. "Where are we?"

"Shh, go to sleep," Mrs. Breslo tells her, smoothing the sweaty wisps of hair away from her face.

"Sarina," Mrs. Breslo says, after she has found

three large candles in the kitchen drawer and lit them with a match. "How long have you been all alone in this house?"

The candle flame moves fluidly in the darkness, casting a quiet glow about the room.

"Only three days," I say. Mrs. Breslo looks at me in that tender way that mothers look at their children after they have fallen down, or are about to cry. Something stirs deep inside my aching place, but I shrug it away. "Thomas Scott and Te Te are here during the day," I tell her. "I'm never alone."

"But aren't you?" she says, placing one hand against my cheek and holding it there for a moment. Her hand is soft, like a dove, and I do not move away.

An hour later, Mr. Breslo returns. Oldman Jacob, his head now wrapped in a white bandage, steps carefully out of the car while Mr. Breslo holds his arm to steady him.

"Is he okay?" I ask.

"He's fine," Mr. Breslo replies. He leads Oldman to his wooden chair and gently sits him down. Oldman is awake but looks strange, as if he is looking at a picture that he cannot understand.

"Oh, thank God," Mrs. Breslo breathes a long sigh of relief.

"Oldman," I say, shaking him by the shoulder.

"He's sedated from the painkillers," Mr. Breslo explains. "But the doctor said he'll be fine in a few hours. You should keep an eye on him for the rest of"—he pauses and looks at his watch—"the morning."

"How many stitches did they give him?" Mrs. Breslo wants to know.

"Seventeen."

"Poor man."

"I get my whipper an' my chopper," Oldman murmurs from the chair.

"All the way home," Mr. Breslo laughs. "Whippers and choppers."

"They're his favorite things," I say. Mr. and Mrs. Breslo look at each other, and suddenly I feel uncomfortable.

"You can go home now," I tell them. "I mean, thank you for everything."

Mr. Breslo scratches the back of his neck and glances at Mrs. Breslo.

"I don't like the idea of leaving a little girl all by herself," she tells her husband. "What if those thieves come back?"

"They won't," Mr. Breslo says. "It's just about daylight and they were probably frightened out of their minds by Oldman Jacob's"—he stops and chuckles—"whippers and choppers."

"I'm fine, really," I say again. "Honest."

Mrs. Breslo looks unconvinced, but when Mr. Breslo starts the car, it is clear the decision has been made. So she goes back into the house to collect her daughter.

"Are we going home now?" Katrina asks sleepily, leaning her head on her mother's shoulder as she gets into the car.

"Yes, sweetheart," Mrs. Breslo says, pressing her lips to Katrina's forehead. An emptiness widens inside my chest, and I look away.

Mr. Breslo leans across his wife and daughter, and rolls down the passenger-side window. "Call us if you need anything," he says loudly, over the sound of the car engine.

"I will." The veranda lights switch on by themselves suddenly, and I can hear the groan of the air conditioners starting up again inside the house. I wave as the car backs down the path and disappears around a turn.

I sit on the stone veranda tile for a long time,

watching Oldman. Gradually his eyes take in his surroundings, piecing everything back together.

"Does it hurt?" I ask him.

"No-o," he says slowly.

"I'm glad you're not dead," I tell him.

"Yeh."

"Thank you for saving me from the rogues," I say.

"Yeh."

Oldman reaches for his pipe in his bag. He lights it, expelling slow puffs of smoke, and together we watch the sun slowly awaken from its long night's sleep, gently lifting itself above the dusty gray blanket of early morning and coloring the yard with yellow.

CHAPTER 13

The Rush
of Spirit

My parents are returning from Ghana tomorrow, and I am arguing with Te Te.

"I told you, I'm leaving," I say. "Boima is taking me to Chugbor to meet his family."

"You gal not finish school study. You actin' jes' like chicken, you scratch on this side, you scratch on that side, every day you ain' do nothin'. Wha' I comin' tell you ma now?"

"I don't care. Just tell her I did everything. She won't check."

"Lie? You want I mus' lie on my job?" Te Te's eyes harden in anger.

"Why not? It wouldn't be the first time."

When I say this, Te Te's posture slackens and her definition fades, like a sand castle hit by an ocean wave. She knows I am referring to the stolen jar of boney fish, safely tucked away beneath my mattress, my hold, my power over her.

"Sarina," Te Te says, crossing her forearms so tightly the ridges of her muscles twitch beneath the skin. "Someday all you eye will open an' you will understand that plenty thing big pass you."

"I don't know what you're talking about," I say.

"Ehn't you know sometime the ocean so quiet you can hear the fish sing they underwater song?" she asks me, her tone softening a little.

"Maybe."

"An' different time sea so frisky it want eat everyone who go inside?"

I nod, remembering.

"Sometime," Te Te says, leaning so close to me that her soap smell, clean as winter air, drifts around me, "on the other side the ocean, lagoon water start to cross the sand. In the begin jes' a small-small stream movin' to the sea. But soon stream change to river, an' river change to heavy flood that crumble an' divide the sand. Soon, whole lagoon goin' hurry-hurry for the sea, an' sea get vex at lagoon. It big an' lagoon small, an' sea fini swallow lagoon one time. Lagoon never know wha' happen befo' it empty, gone, jes' like that, inside the sea."

"So?" I say, "Who cares?" I do not tell Te Te that a buzzing vibration travels along my spinal column at the thought of the lagoon splitting apart the beach in a headlong rush toward the thrashing sea. I do not tell her that I would like to see this.

"Ehn't you see," Te Te continues in a voice that echoes either a warning or a plea, "you the lagoon. That you the rush o' spirit movin' to the big-big sea. You too small, an' still you goin' straight for something big like sea. An' when the ocean fini drink everything down, you the one comin' be empty, small gal, jes' like lagoon. That you the one." Te Te takes a step away from me and shakes her head, as if my presence alone were a bad omen that would bring ill fate to others.

"I'm not listening to you," I call after her as she walks away, although the edges of my mind feel frayed and there is a jarring sensation in my bones. What great force lies in the beyond that will empty my spirit as the vast ocean swallows the lagoon? I do not want to think about it and am glad when Boima arrives to take me up the path to Old Road where we will visit his family in Chugbor.

Boima's house is in a little village at the top of an orange-colored hill, where roofs are made of corrugated tin and walls are held together with mud and straw. As my feet walk upon sand bordering the village, I can already hear the clattering of utensils and the twittering of children over the hollow pounding of the cassava root inside a mortar and pestle. When we reach Boima's home, he calls out in a language that skims across the air like skipping stones on water, and four children run out from inside the house.

Boima introduces his three small brothers to me, Mulbah, Boakai, and Pewu, and his big sister Kolu, who looks about fourteen. Kolu smiles shyly at me, but the little ones touch my pale feet and check their fingertips, as if my skin were made of the fine powder on a butterfly's wing. Then Boima chases his brothers away and they scatter in three directions, squealing and giggling. Kolu's stare travels upward from my sandals to the pattern on my dress before resting on my hair, which sways as easily in the breeze as the gauzy threads of a spider's web.

"Where's your ma?" I ask Kolu, looking at a gray pot outside a wooden lean-to, left alone to boil over a smoky fire. The scent of wood and smoke wafts through the air, but it is not unpleasant.

"She comin' back jes' now, she gone to buy some groun' pea."

"Oh." I look at Kolu's mocha skin, her eyes that reflect the joyfulness of the sun, and suddenly I feel odd, out of place, aware of my thin, wispy hair that cannot match the beauty of Kolu's country plat. "Your hair is so pretty," I tell her after a moment. "Who did it?"

"That my ma," Kolu says. I can see her fingers itch to feel the texture of my hair, so dull and lifeless next to her own.

"I can plat you hair," she says softly, and then quickly adds, "if you want it."

"Really?" I ask, doubtful that my brittle hair would conform to the sturdy weave that so many Liberian girls adorn with colorful beads and ribbons.

"Yeh. I can make a bohnswe plat," she says thoughtfully, holding the soft hair and inspecting it under the light with an experienced eye.

"What's that?" I ask.

But Kolu doesn't answer me. Instead she sits me down upon a log in front of the lean-to and the boiling pot and removes a comb from her dress pocket. She parts my hair and gathers the strands together between skilled fingers.

"Ow," I yell as she twists the hair over and under along the side of my head, just above the ear.

"Sorry, yah," Kolu says.

"S'okay."

"How did you learn to plat hair?" I ask, my head bent down and tilted to the side so all I can see are the dark cracks in the wooden log and the ash-colored sand.

"That my ma show."

"Oh. Do you work in Joe Bar too?" I ask her.

"No-o. I workin' Rally Time Market.

"What do you sell?"

"Kinja."

"What's that?"

"That big-big basket woman them carry on they back."

119

"You can make those?" I am impressed.

"Yeh. I like workin' with my hand. Ma say from time I was small-small child my finger fini itchin' to make all kind of something."

"Do you sell a lot of kinja at Rally Time?"

"Sometime yes, sometime no." Kolu pulls so hard on my hair I can feel the roots lifting up the scalp. "But my ma, she say, 'That one who respec' the river can catch the fish.' If you get kind heart an' you love, good-good thing comin' to you."

I think this over while Kolu works on my hair. I am not so sure I agree. If nothing bad happens to those with kind hearts, then why did Oldman Jacob get attacked by rogues? How come a person as unkind as Katrina is allowed to have a pet monkey, and why does my own mother look at me with unseeing eyes?

After a long while, Kolu finishes and leads me into the house, where a stained yellow curtain divides two windowless rooms with low ceilings and smooth dirt floors. The boys' room contains nothing more than two thin mattresses and a pile of gray sheets, but in Kolu's room, which she shares with her mother, there is a rectangular mirror lying on a wooden dresser. Kolu holds the mirror up to my face and I am startled when I see my reflection, a grinning girl whose fly-away hair is now pulled back and divided into even corn rows, fastened at the ends with shiny blue and green beads. I am astonished and pleased at the change in my appearance and gaily exclaim, "I love it!" to Kolu, who smiles proudly at me in the mirror.

Just then, a tall woman enters the room. She places both hands on her hips and flashes us a smile so welcoming I am sure she has mistaken us for the rainbow arc that holds up the sky after a long rain. I look into eyes that brim with happiness and light and see Boima all over again.

"You gal," she says to me, smiling still. "You lookin' jes' like Liberian child now. You an' Kolu, you resemble." Her laughter has a richness and a depth that seems to fill the darkest corners of the room.

"Kolu did it."

Again, the eyes light up with the pure, clean joy of living, of the richness of the colors of sun and earth, of moon and rain. I have never in my life met anyone whose presence alone feels like such a celebration.

"I'm Sarina," I tell her.

"I know." She beams, taking one of my hands between both of hers. "I know plenty thing 'bout you, you gal."

"You do?" I ask, surprised.

Boima's ma reaches forward and picks a piece of lint out of Kolu's hair before continuing. "That you ain' get no brother, no sister, jes' you livin' by you own self in one big-big house the other side of Ol' Road."

"It's all right." I shrug, not wanting her to feel sorry for me. But Boima's ma pushes us out of the house and into the afternoon sunlight, where she pulls the wooden log up closer to the fire and motions for me to sit down.

"No, small gal," she says, lifting up the pot cover and glancing inside. "It not all right. Ehn't you know God give us two something, that work, an' that play. An' my boy, Boima, he a good-good boy, but ever since he was small-small he fini forget 'bout play. Every day he in worry fo' something. Worry fo' market business, worry fo' basket money, worry he small-small brother not get rice to fill he hongry gut. But I say, lion pekin got to play inside the tall grass befo' he grow big and run to catch deer." She pauses then, and dips a spoon into a simmering red sauce before continuing. "Now Boima, he was grow too quick-quick from the worry, an' he fini loss he smile. Then he meet you an' one more time he find he happy face. So I thank you too much fo' that one there. Thank you too much-o." She closes her eyes and blows lightly on the sauce before tasting it. Then she tosses some hot peppers inside the pot and replaces the cover once more.

"It's really Boima who's been a good friend to *me*," I say. But Boima's ma waves my words away with her hands as if they were small bugs in the twilight air. "That nothin', you gal," she says. "My boy Boima workin' too much, but even a river get dry sometime an' need help from the rain. You was help us in the dry time and we thank you too much for that one there."

I ponder these words, feeling slightly bewildered. How exactly have I helped Boima? Then, quite naturally, Kolu takes out something from behind a tin bowl that pulls out my spirit in such a rush that I very nearly gasp for breath. I blink rapidly in the afternoon light, hoping that each time I open my eyes the image in front of me will disappear. But it keeps returning. Boney fish. I am staring at a half-empty jar of boney fish.

CHAPTER 14

The Sting
of the Bee

"You lied to me," I explode at Boima as I march along the path after running down the orange-colored hill, away from Boima's village. "How could you lie to me?"

"I not lie-o." The answer comes quietly, from behind me.

"Yes, you did. You and Te Te stole from us and that's just the same as lying." I chew on the insides of my cheek and kick up dirt with my sandals as I hurry to stay ahead of Boima.

"Sarina," Boima says, breathing heavily as he struggles to keep up with me on the path. "Wait small."

"How could you be on Te Te's side," I continue, "when you know how much I hate her!"

"Sarina," Boima repeats, "I not choosin' to one side o' the other. Ehn't you know it jes' my gut was empty same time my heart was full up. That hongry make a boy do all kind o' something."

"You didn't have to steal," I answer coldly. "You could have asked me. I'm your friend. I would have helped."

"Ehn't you know that my pride too big fo' that one there? That shame make it I never ask nobody fo' nothin'."

"I wouldn't have cared," I say, staring ahead at the dense green leaves that color the edges of the narrow path. "All this time you and Te Te were keeping a secret from me."

"She was jes' helpin me an' my family, that all."

I whirl around on the path and face Boima. He looks small, a weary figure against a wide background of thick green trees and fading sun.

"You can't be friends with both of us," I say, looking at him through eyes of cold blue glass. "It's either one or the other, so who are you going to choose?"

"Green sea turtle not able decide between the ocean for swimmin' an' the outside air for breathin'. Need all two for live," he answers quietly.

"Fine," I say. "Have it your way. I'm going home." Anger sticks inside my throat, making it difficult for me to form the words. "And don't follow me. I don't want to see you anymore. Not now, not ever."

Boima looks at me sorrowfully as a bus rushes past us, its tires kicking up red dust particles to mingle with the motor's cough of exhaust along the roadside.

"I mean it," I say, leaving him to stand motionless amid the roiling dust clouds, his body held still against the thinness of the tropical wind. I hurry along the path toward home, hoping that the swiftness of my feet will seal the trembling crack inside my chest that threatens to empty out my soul. A tornado of images spirals across my mind, memories of Te Te standing beneath the mango tree, looking secretive and guilty, images of a jar of boney fish inside the pocket of a blue sweater, inside the palm of Kolu's hand. How dare Boima betray me and side with Te Te, the enemy! Boima was my friend and mine only, not to be shared, not meant to be taken from me by anyone, least of all Te Te.

I am so preoccupied with my anger and hurt at Boima that when I reach the swinging gate outside my house I almost do not notice my parents' car, parked squarely in the driveway. Immediately my insides fill with a numbing fear. How can they be home already? Weren't they supposed to return tomorrow? I hasten up the path and find my parents and Mrs. Breslo standing awkwardly on the veranda, my father's suitcase and my mother's leather travel bag placed between them. Apparently they have just come home. Early.

"Oh, Sarina," Mrs. Breslo greets me warmly as I approach. "I just thought I'd stop by to say hello to find out how you were doing all by yourself. Aren't I lucky that your parents happened to come home this very moment?"

My father raises his eyebrows at me in acknowledgment, but my mother frowns, and in a quiet tone that only hints at its sharp edges, says, "Where have you been?"

"Just around." My mother's gray eyes look dull, and she is paler, thinner. Right away I understand that the trip to Ghana has not made any difference in her health.

"You have a very courageous daughter," Mrs. Breslo says, hurrying to fill the empty spaces in the air with a rush of words. She smiles nervously at me and continues, "I was just telling your parents how you saved Oldman Jacob's life the other night. To think what might have happened if she hadn't awakened," Mrs. Breslo says, looking uncertainly at my parents. She blinks rapidly, snapping and unsnapping the little metal clasp on her purse.

"Sarina is very practical," my father says, glancing at my mother for a moment, who nods in silent agreement and smiles thinly at Mrs. Breslo. "We have always been able to rely on her in times of . . . emergency." He rests a heavy hand upon my shoulder. My mother says nothing.

"You can imagine our surprise when we found her all by herself—"

"I wasn't by myself," I interrupt. My mother sways a little, ever so slightly, and grasps the wooden arm of Oldman's chair to steady herself. My father notices and moves closer to her.

"Well, practically." Mrs. Breslo smiles uneasily at my parents. She waits for them to respond. But they do not say anything more.

"Well, I guess I'd better be on my way. You must have some unpacking to do. . . ." The heaviness of the air wraps around Mrs. Breslo, engulfing her words in a thick, uncomfortable silence. She looks at my mother for a moment.

"Thank you for helping us with Oldman Jacob," my father says, reaching into his wallet and pulling out a few bills. "For the hospital and your trouble."

"Oh, no trouble," she says, although she takes the cash and puts it inside her purse. Then, with nothing more to say, she extends a friendly little wave in my direction and hurries down the path, leaving me alone with my parents inside the silence, to wait for the reprimand. But none comes.

"Good job, Sarina," my father tells me, as he takes my mother's arm and leads her into the house. "I see you've managed very well without us."

"It wasn't a big deal," I say, following behind.

"Where were you?" my mother asks me again as my father leads her carefully down the hallway. "And who did that to your hair?"

My hand reaches up to my head. The bohnswe plat. I had forgotten.

"Where are Te Te and Thomas Scott?" she demands to know.

"They're in the kitchen," my father tells her soothingly. "Now I want you to rest awhile before dinner. I'll talk to Sarina."

My mother nods and lies down on the bed, but she does not close her eyes until they have silently connected with my own. My father covers her with a thin sheet and motions for me to follow him back down the hallway toward the front room, where we sit down on two armless wooden chairs. Again I am quiet, and wait for him to reprimand me for leaving the yard. Again, nothing.

"Sarina." He sighs. "We decided to come back early because she wasn't . . ." He clears his throat, starting again, "Your mother really hasn't been doing very well, has she?"

I shrug my shoulders. "I guess not," I tell him.

"Why didn't you tell me?"

"You were busy. Besides, I can manage." I look squarely into his face.

"Yes," he says, but he looks troubled, as if he has come to a new understanding that he did not want to face. I turn away from him because there are too many other colors in my mind right now, and my head is beginning to hurt. Te Te. My mother. Boima. The boney fish.

"I think we are going to have to make some changes," my father says slowly, standing up and walking over to a window overlooking one side of the yard. "But first I have to go back to the bush for a week or so, to straighten things out." He turns back to me, and looks into my eyes, almost pleadingly. "Would you mind . . . taking care of things a little while longer?"

"Okay," I answer. I feel dull and flat, as lifeless as a wooden board.

"That's my Sarina," he says, breathing out a long sigh of relief and placing one hand on my head for a moment. "I've always been able to count on you, haven't I?"

I nod, but I am not really listening to him. I am thinking of Boima and the half-empty jar of

132

boney fish behind the tin bowl inside a lean-to in Chugbor. I am seeing Te Te looking up inside the leaves of the mango tree, the missing jars on pantry shelves, and I feel a crack climbing up my insides, threatening to split wide open the dry wood of my spirit.

"I'll be back in a week," my father says, and then he is swiftly out the door and returning his suitcase to the inside of the car. I sit in the front room for a while, long after the engine's thrum has echoed and faded into the heavy stillness of the air. Then I walk into the kitchen, where Thomas Scott is thinly chopping a plantain and dropping the coin-shaped slices into a vat of boiling oil.

"Where is Te Te?" I ask him. He points to the window with his knife and resumes chopping. I exit the kitchen and head into the backyard, where Te Te is hanging laundry on a clothesline by the almond tree.

"Te Te."

She spins around, startled.

"I know what you did. You stole the boney fish to give to Boima."

Te Te does not answer. She returns to the laundry basket and lifts out a red T-shirt. She fastens it to the line with two wooden clothes-pins.

"Why?" I ask her, blinking uncomprehendingly. "Why did you do that?"

"Why?" she repeats after me, as if she cannot fathom the question. "Why?" She pulls another piece of clothing from the basket, my mother's yellow dress, and shakes it out, sending a light mist in my direction. "Sarina," she says, "not everything so simple like you thinkin'. Whole world get more color than black an' white."

"But you were keeping secrets with Boima behind my back. He was my friend, not yours."

"Not true. Boima still you friend. Jes' I was help him small. Anyone who spy that boy can see, empty bag can't stand."

I think this over for a moment. It is true that Te Te risked her job to help Boima, and this kindness shows like a dusty speck of starlight through the blackness of my anger. But then the picture of the two of them concealing jars of boney fish and keeping secrets passes over me as the darkness of night sky covers the earth and muffles the stars, and I am suddenly furious all over again.

"You stole from us," I glare at her accusingly. "Stealing is wrong."

Te Te straightens up her shoulders and grips a clothespin tightly, pointing it directly at my heart. "Sometime, a man got to feel the sting o' the bee befo' he can carry honey to the village," she says, leaving me to ponder the wisdom of these words as I storm up the path and into the house.

CHAPTER 15

Golden Lightning

The chairs in the front room are hard. The faded cloth that covers the seat has worn thin, and I can feel the edges of the wood pressing into the space behind my knees. But I do not get up. I am supposed to stay right here, in this straight-backed wooden chair, until my mother has finished speaking to Te Te from behind her bedroom door. I stay, but not because she told me so. I stay because Boima lied to me and is no longer my friend. Because I have no place to go.

But this chair is truly hard. I run my hands forward, along the sides of the wood, and listen as the level tones of my mother's voice carry down the hallway, just barely reaching my ears. But I am too far away, and cannot hear the words inside the sounds. So I push the tip of my index finger into the pointed corner of the chair, where the angles meet, and wonder: How can something be both smooth and sharp at the same time?

I think I am going to stand up. Just for a moment. To stretch. Maybe I will take a few steps down the hallway, toward my mother's bedroom. Just to move my legs around. Yes, this is what I will do.

There is a bookshelf against the wall, just outside my mother's bedroom door. The door hangs slightly ajar, and a thin line of sunlight escapes through the narrow crack, brightening a strip of hallway tiles. I carefully balance one knee upon the beam of light and lay a finger across the spines of books along the shelf. Is it my fault that I can hear the words now, as I choose a book to bring back to the wooden chair?

"You aren't watching her closely enough," I hear my mother say accusingly. "You mustn't ever let her out of your sight. She can't be racing from the yard every time I turn my back to rest."

"Fo' true," Te Te answers, but her voice sounds unfamiliar, too soft, as if weakened by the lingering echo of my mother's words.

"It is difficult for a healthy person to understand what it means to be sick all of the time," she continues. "What it means to always need someone. But Sarina knows. She has always known."

"Yeh."

I can see them so clearly inside my mind, as if there were no door at all to separate me from the images on the other side. My mother is leaning back on the pillows against the headboard. Her arms lie at her sides in two straight lines, over sheets that are pulled up to her chest. She is trying not to move too much because her sugar levels are now high, and she feels sick.

And Te Te is looking everywhere around the room—at the end table by the door, at the bookshelves along the wall, at the writing desk by the farthest window—everywhere but into the gray eyes of my mother. The unseeing eyes of my mother.

"Sarina has always been like 'golden lightning,'" my mother says in a voice she reserves for quoting poetry. "She has always felt it necessary to 'discover stars, and sail in the wind's eye . . .'"

The marble floor is cold against my knee. I

138

lay one hand upon the door and hold it there. The hinges creak a little and I hold my breath.

"Now Te Te, I know that Sarina is off making friends, running I don't know where, but the fact of the matter is, I am unwell, and cannot share her with anyone. She is mine and mine only . . ."

Something about those words. They press upon the underside of my skin, like old bones.

". . . so do not fail in your responsibilities. I would suffer little remorse at relieving you of your duties if you cannot hold up your end." Her words are so sharp they seem to splinter her own voice, like a crack that travels up thinnest glass.

Te Te is silent. I remove my hand from the door and flatten myself against the bookshelf. The ridges of the wood make indentations in my back and it hurts. But I do not care. Something worse is hurting from the inside, a feeling I cannot place.

The door opens and a figure fills the empty space. Te Te. She does not see me right away and I am struck by how different she looks, like an old tree after a heavy rain. She turns to meet my stare, and for a brief second I am reminded of Ticky, of the tiny bamboo cage and those eyes looking out at me. But before I can think of something to say, Te Te walks past me, holding herself perfectly upright as she follows the straight line back down the marble hallway, as if she were balancing an invisible basket upon her head.

I turn around and look inside the bedroom. My mother is not in bed at all. She is standing in front of the dresser, grasping the edge with one hand for support. She is looking the other way, out the window, and does not see me. Against the backdrop of the dark wooden dresser, she looks flat and colorless in her white nightgown, like a black-and-white photograph.

Why does my mother have to be this way? Again, the angular shape of words press sharply against my insides, rising painfully to the surface of my mind—*not to be shared . . . mine and mine only . . . who are you going to choose . . . bone at my bone . . . I cannot share you with anyone*—until I cannot stand to hear them anymore, to hear myself inside my mother's voice. How can this be? How can our voices be the same?

The sleeves of my mother's nightgown are wrinkled, and she carefully removes her hand from the dresser to smooth them down, straightening out the lines. First one, and then the other. She curls a few loose strands of hair back around one ear.

Am I like her? Is the whole world so simple that all one has to do is smooth out wrinkles and straighten lines? I look at my mother standing in front of me in her nightgown, in front of her dresser. *Whole world get more color than black an' white.*

No. This cannot be. It will not be. I do not want my words to echo hers. I want to be different. I will be different.

I have to go now. I must find Boima. He will understand when I tell him that I am sorry. That I made a mistake and am not angry anymore. Probably he will smile and say, "N'mind yah," and then we will stir red dust upon papaya leaves as we race along the old roads to Rally Time Market, where I will buy a golden plum. I have heard that they are sweet. But first I have to find him. I have to find him now.

"Sarina." My mother notices me in the doorway and takes a few careful steps forward, reaching just far enough to close her fingers around my wrist, drawing me in.

"Stay with me," she says, pulling me closer. She holds on tightly, but I am thinking of that day in the lagoon, my hand around Boima's wrist as I pulled him to the sand, out of the water.

My mother cries out as I pull myself free of her and run as fast as I am able, back down the marble hallway and toward the front door that pushes out into the heat of the yard. Feet upon stone tiles, feet upon soft earth, I am caught up in my own rhythm now, and I smile to myself when I realize that my mother was right about one thing. I am just like golden lightning. And I am sailing in the wind's eye as I head for the gate which will no longer keep me from finding Boima if I just reach forward and push up the latch with one—

Hand. One hand. It falls heavily upon my shoulder and grips me tightly, jerking me backward. I spin around, and my breath rushes back in, fast, when I see her. Te Te. I am looking into the sad, dark eyes of Te Te.

CHAPTER 16

I Hold Your Foot

So I am left here, beneath African sky, tied to a tree. Again. My mother is much worse now, and the reactions come faster, so every day she ties me to the gate, to Oldman's wooden chair, to the mango tree.

Sometimes, while my mother is sleeping, I beg for Te Te to let me leave the yard, so that I might find Boima. I promise her that I will come back right away, before my mother awakens, before she even realizes that I have gone. But Te Te is afraid now, and will not let me go. And Boima does not come. So there is nothing left for me to do except tilt the senses backward in my mind to find the gray marbled surface of the swaying ocean, the spicy whiff of palm butter simmering over burning stones, the touch of velvet sunlight on my face in early morning, before the heat moves in.

I am thinking and remembering today when suddenly I open my eyes and find a visitor standing behind the gate to the yard. Kolu. She slips past the gate and stands in front of me, trembling on a patch of grass below the mango tree, looking wilted and afraid.

"Kolu, what's the matter?" I ask. "What are you doing here?"

"Boima," she says, in a voice quieter than wind passing through leaves.

"What about Boima?"

"He—" She pauses and breathes in, very slowly. "He too sick."

My heart jumps. "Sick?" I ask. "From what?"

But Kolu cannot answer me. She shakes her head and tears fall from her eyes like drops of rain.

"Kolu," I nearly yell, panicked now. "You have to tell me, what's the matter with Boima?"

"He too sick, too sick," she echoes herself almost madly, pressing her fingers to her eyes as if to hold back a leaking dam of tears. "Sarina, you got to help us. Help my brother," she cries, gathering strength from somewhere within, long enough to remove her hands from her face and look at me with frightened eyes. "I beg you, Sarina, I beg you. Help us."

"Okay," I tell her, glancing toward the house for a second. Nobody is outside. Yet. But my mother never leaves me tied for long, and will be returning any moment to cut me loose. We do not have much time.

"Kolu, I can't do anything unless you untie me from this tree. Get me free and I promise I'll help you."

Kolu nods and stops crying, lightly touching her fingertips to the knotted twine as if she were just noticing that I am tied to the mango tree. She begins to work on the most unforgiving knot, picking nimbly at the angry snarls of twine with delicate fingers.

"It's no use," I tell her after a few minutes and no sign of release. "You're going to have to find a knife, or a pair of scissors."

But Kolu doesn't answer me. Her fingers work rapidly in a blur of grace and speed as agile as the spider's dance across web strings. But she is not moving fast enough. With a drowning heart I suddenly hear the muted call of my mother from deep inside the house.

"*Sarina!*"

"Hurry, Kolu," I whisper tightly. "My mother is coming."

"*I'm coming to untie you, Sarina. I'm so sorry.*"

Kolu's chin hardens and her lips turn down in concentrated effort as tears flow in thin rivers from her eyes, but still she does not remove her fingers from the twine. The trees seem to jerk in rhythm with the pounding of my heart as I imagine my mother walking down the cool hallway, moving steadily in the direction of the front door. She would be approaching the door carefully, perhaps lingering at the handle for a few moments before leaning into the heavy wood frame and pushing into the stagnant heat of the outdoors. She would be treading lightly along the veranda tiles, holding a pair of scissors—

And then Kolu pulls her hands back and the twine leaps and catches a glimmer of light before dropping limply over the roots of the tree and I am free, sprinting past the gate with Kolu, away from the reverberating cries of my mother and running toward Old Road and the orange-colored hill that will lead me to Chugbor, where Boima is sick and waiting for me to help him.

The first thing I notice when we reach the village is the awful quiet. There are no children laughing in between the steady beat of a mortar and pestle, no spattering fire beneath a whispering pot of palm sauce. Even the sand around the yard holds the silence in a suffocating breath that voices cannot penetrate.

Kolu moves aside the hanging yellow curtain inside the house. At first all I can see is a gray film of darkness, but gradually my eyes adjust to the poor light and I see Mulbah, Boakai, and Pewu sitting in a little half circle on the floor. The room is dismally quiet, except for the rise and fall of Pewu's tiny breath as he weeps large tears onto the smooth dirt floor. And then I see him. Boima. He is in the corner by the farthest wall, just past the pile of gray sheets, next to the mattresses. He is sitting upright on a thin straw mat with legs folded and arms hanging loosely at his sides. He is emaciated, so ghastly thin that the skin wraps tightly around his body, outlining the details of his bones. His jaw hangs open in an eerie accidental smile and his eyes stare directly into my face without seeing, as if I were an open window, a slice of air. His face, once the shade of sunlight on a flash of copper, has faded to a sickening hue, a sallow tone the color of withered leaves, of ancient teeth. Yellow.

"What's wrong with him?" I cry out, rushing forward and shaking him by the shoulder. But his head just teeters back and forth like a wobbly top and his arms feel as brittle as pieces of driftwood.

"Boima, say something," I plead, but his eyes are so dark they look almost black, as if someone had reached into his soul and turned out the light.

"Kolu," I say, without turning around. "Why doesn't he talk?"

"Yellow fever." I turn around and find Boima's ma standing behind me. Her form no longer fills the room. The smile is gone, her eyes are dim, and she looks broken, ruined, the rainbow colors of her spirit dissolved into a gray and forlorn despair. "My boy get yellow fever," she sobs, folding into herself like a great dying bird and sinking to the floor in desolate anguish.

Yellow fever. Boima has yellow fever. No, it cannot be. Not now, not here. Yellow fever was for a woman named Sarzah, a person I had never seen. It is not for someone I know, someone who is my best friend. It is not for a boy called Boima. I will not let this happen.

A haunting wail erupts into the stillness as Boima's ma lets out a cry, longer and deeper than anything I have ever heard from a human before. It is a sound you could almost touch, the textured pain of grief, and I feel as if my heart is being crushed as Boima's ma half walks, half crawls on her knees toward me until she is level with my feet. She reaches forward with elbows pressed against the dirt and gently eases off one sandal, pushing it aside to wrap her hands around my foot in the humblest plea a Liberian can ever hope to make. It is the softest calling, a whispered prayer.

"Help us," she begins, looking at me through eyes lost inside an ocean of desperation. "I hold you foot, Sarina. I hold you foot."

I nod. And then I turn and run out of the house, through the little village and down the orange-colored hill, trying hard not to imagine what could happen to Boima if I don't get help fast. My breath tears at the edges of my insides while I run and run, until at last I am pushing aside the gate and screaming for Te Te to come quickly and help me.

"Where you gone?" she asks me, almost wildly, as I heave on the veranda, barely able to breathe. "Ehn't you know I comin' loss my job if you run away like that?"

"It's Boima," I gasp. My lungs feel heavy, as if I had inhaled the dampness with the air. "He's sick and we have to get help right now."

"Wha' you talkin', sick?"

"I mean, he's really sick. He's got—" I shudder, thinking if I avoid the words they might not really be true. "Yellow fever."

"Ayah, my people," Te Te murmurs, and drops the paring knife she had been using to skin a guava. It makes a hollow sound when it hits the tiles.

"We have to help him now!"

"Sarina, we can't do that one there."

"Why not? What are you talking about?" I ask. My heart feels as if it is dropping to my stomach.

"That boy too sick. He need American doctor man. Me part, I can't do nothin'."

"What do you mean? Can't we take him to Cooper Clinic?"

"Ain' get no ride, small-gal. Anyway, ehn't you know Cooper Clinic no good for that one there? That boy need to go for American Embassy quick-quick, get the medicine."

"But they won't treat him there!" I shout suddenly, remembering Thomas Scott and the nurse with the bifocals.

Te Te nods, looks at me, and voices what I am already thinking. "We can't do nothin' right now-o," she says quietly. "That you pa we need."

"Well, when's he coming home?"

"Evenin' time, maybe."

"That could be too late! We have to go now!"

But Te Te only shakes her head. "Sarina, I can't leave you ma by she own self."

"Where's Thomas Scott?"

"He gone to the market. He gone buy juice.

After you run away you ma was too mix up in the head, an' she was vex. Then Thomas Scott give the juice and she drink the whole thing. Now she sleepin'."

But I am only listening to Te Te with one ear. I cannot think about my mother right now, when my inner eye is seeing the thin shell of a boy sitting upon a yellow mat in grayest darkness. Not when I know that boy is supposed to be Boima but does not look like him. Not when I am the only person who can help him. The only one.

"Te Te," I begin, feeling truly low for what I am about to say. But what choice do I have? I am now a part of something huge and overwhelming, much larger than myself, and I must struggle against it or lose.

"If you don't help me save Boima," I say, hating the voice that carries these words, "then I am going to tell my mother about the boney fish." I do not want to threaten her like this, but there is no other way. I cannot save Boima without her help.

Te Te bends down and picks up the knife from the veranda. Her fingers form a clenched fist around the handle, and when she straightens up her wooden eyes have caught on fire, and for a brief moment I wonder if she is going to attack me. But she doesn't. She holds her arms solidly at her sides and stares, charring my insides with her fury.

"Go 'head," she says, daring me with her eyes. "Go tell you ma."

I had not expected this reaction, and do not know how to respond.

"Go tell you ma," Te Te continues, her voice searing with anger, "that I the one fini take from the house that get more food in the pantry than every house in every village in Liberia. Go 'head, tell you ma. An' don't forget to tell that I steal the boney fo' you friend, 'cause all two you eye was close and not see the boy too dry."

She moves toward me, but I take a step backward, away from her. I have never seen Te Te so angry.

"Ehn't you know I was see you an' that boy hidin' inside the mango tree from the first time? An' why I not fini run to you ma, now, run to tell her you lettin' one Liberian boy inside the

yard? Why I not tell you ma? Why?" She grabs
my elbow and looks me in the face, waiting for
the answer.

"I . . . I don't know," I stammer.

"I jes' close all two my eye, jes' close my mouth
'cause I know small gal got to have friend, she
can't stay whole day by her one. Warm soup got
to fill the empty bowl. That the way o' the
world fo' true. Jes' like that the way fo' hongry
boy to eat when he get the hongry gut. I try to
help in my own way"—her voice raises in pitch
then, and she nearly chokes out the next few
words as her eyes fill with tears—" 'cause I love
that boy Boima jes' like he my own child, like
sun love the day and moon the night. Ehn't you
know I want try to keep that boy from goin' to
God befo' he time? Ehn't you know? But I got
to keep my job. I can not loss my job."

She covers her mouth with her hands as if
trying to contain the rising sobs that rock her
body, but she cannot arrest the tears that fill
and flow, and fill again.

I stand on the veranda, watching Te Te cry.
Powerful waves of feeling sweep across my
mind, each rushing forward to overtake the next.
I am both angry and terrified that Te Te will

154

not help me, although now I can feel something new and disturbing rise to the surface. Shame. I am ashamed, deeply ashamed, and do not know what to say, so I decide to say nothing at all. I sit down on the edge of the veranda and listen to the sound of Te Te's tears and wait for my father to return. There is nothing else to do.

CHAPTER 17

Empty as Air

It is almost dark when my father finally returns home. He pulls in the driveway and switches off the ignition. His face is long and filled with lines.

"Dad," I cry, jumping up from where I have been dozing in and out of nightmarish sleep, next to Te Te, on the veranda floor. "Boima has yellow fever. You have to make the doctor at the American Embassy—"

"Who is Boima?" my father asks, getting out of the car.

"He's my friend. Please, Dad, we need your help."

"Where is your mother?" he asks, glancing at Te Te, who is standing beside me, her eyes reflecting the faded light of evening.

"She sleepin', bossman," Te Te says. "She gone to bed after lunch."

"Dad, please help us," I say. My voice feels thin and fragile, as if it might break at any moment.

"Maybe tomorrow," my father says wearily. "It's getting late. We can see about your friend in the morning."

"Tomorrow that boy will be dead." Te Te's voice cuts sharply across the gray dusk on the veranda, and my father stiffens before turning his head to meet her rigid stare. He looks at her pensively for a long moment.

"All right, Sarina," he says quietly, still looking at Te Te. "We'll take him to Cooper Clinic."

"But Te Te says—"

"And I say," he interrupts, without removing his eyes from Te Te, "that we will take him to Cooper Clinic."

I show my father which way to turn as the car tires crunch over pebbles, straining inside the potholes along the uneven path.

"How do you know the way?" he asks me as the car pitches and creaks its way up the orange-colored hill. I shrug my shoulders and look out the car window. How can I begin to explain a boy called Boima, who once smiled at the sunlight but now sits inside a dark room with eyes snuffed out like candle flames. How can I explain to my father that I need the chance to tell Boima that I am sorry, that I was selfish and I didn't understand, that Te Te is not an enemy but maybe even a friend. How can I explain these things to my father now, inside the quiet echo of a stilled car motor while outside I can hear the sound of—

Voices. A strange chorus of wailing voices looms high above the roofs of houses in the little village, coloring the air with a black and terrifying sound. The cries are wild and frenzied, twisting over and under each other in a near-delirious unleashing of something terrible and incomprehensible and I hate it, hate it with a fierceness and a fury. I roll up the car window and clamp both hands over my ears to stifle the ugly, awful noise.

"Stay here," my father says firmly, getting out of the car. I squeeze my eyes tightly shut until I can see the gray shadow of my father carrying Boima in my mind. We would be rushing Boima to Cooper Clinic soon, where the missionaries there will find a way to fix Boima so that his face will radiate with the glow of his spirit, so that he will once more smile at me with sunlit eyes.

But then the driver's side door is opening and my father has returned. He is not carrying Boima. He sits down and looks out through the windshield without starting the car. Silently, he traces his finger around the bottom half of the steering wheel, stopping every so often to reverse direction. Back. Forth. Up. Down.

"Is he all right?" I ask, thinking perhaps my father came back so quickly because he saw that he did not need to bring Boima to the car. That Boima got better on his own. But a deeper part of me knows this cannot be so.

"Sarina," my father says, turning his head to look at me in such a way that I know Boima is not all right, that he will never be all right again. "I'm sorry . . ." He pauses and takes a very quiet breath. "All of this happened so quickly—"

I look away and stare out the window, feeling nothing. Absolutely nothing. My father starts the car and backs down the hill and all the while he is talking I do not listen and I do not hear. Sounds form to take the shape of words that are meant to reach my ears, but I continue to look out the window into the black nothing of night, feeling nothing because I am nothing. I am like the wind between leaves, as hollow as the bones of a bird, as empty as the air.

When we reach the house, Te Te is waiting on the veranda with Oldman Jacob. They are standing close together, but they are not looking at each other. They are looking at me. My father opens the passenger-side door and I carefully step outside, because now that I have seen Te Te's face I can feel a dangerous tremor starting from within, threatening to create a rift inside me if I move too quickly. My father speaks quietly with Te Te for a moment before glancing at me one more time and then going into the house. Oldman leaves to do his walk about the yard.

I think I can make it to the front door if I move very slowly, with calculated steps, like an old person. Yes, I think I can. My throat is so dry and tight I feel like I am being strangled from the inside, but still, if I move slowly, I think I can make it.

"Sarina." Te Te speaks so quietly, so softly, that for a second I am not sure she has even said my name at all. I lift my eyes to hers and for a moment as thin as a beat in time, I think that I am going to be all right. But then Te Te is holding out her arms to me and I can feel the crack in my chest that I have lived with for so long break wide open, letting go a sea of tears that seems to spring from every corner of my soul.

"It all right, all right," Te Te whispers, pressing me against her clean soap smell as she sways me back and forth to the rhythms of her heartbeat. "Goin' be all right, small gal," she repeats, holding me as I cry an ocean onto her blue kwi dress. We stay that way for a long time, me sobbing and choking out all the anguish of the holding in, her rocking me back and forth like a little lost infant until I have ceased to be my own whole but am a part of her, caught up in an endless current circling around and around, from beginning to end, to beginning again.

CHAPTER 18

Beyond the Mango Tree

We are leaving Africa. My mother does not get out of bed anymore, and my father has made arrangements for me to attend a boarding school in Massachusetts. In New England, my father says, there will be cold autumn air for my mother to breathe, where the leaves will change from green to red, and there will be no tropical heat. There, my mother will have special doctors who will help her to get better, help her to maybe even see me again, the way she used to, a very long time ago.

"We'd like Te Te and Oldman Jacob to work for us," Mr. Breslo is telling my father as I sit on the veranda floor, staring at my sandals.

"That would be fine," my father says. I wonder where Thomas Scott will go, but I do not ask.

"How is Katrina?" my father asks.

Mr. Breslo remarks, "It's funny. A few months ago we bought her a pet monkey. We thought it would teach her about responsibility, but she just wasn't interested. But now, just recently in fact, she has taken a special delight in the thing, playing with it every day, caring for it . . . it's so funny how kids change and grow. . . ."

I walk away then, down the path and across the grass, to where the mango tree stands majestically in the middle of the yard.

"Small gal." I turn around and find Te Te standing behind me.

"Juju," I say, looking into the leaves of the tree.

"Wha' you talkin'?"

"Juju," I tell her. "Boima and I made juju on Katrina and it worked."

"Fo' true." Te Te nods. She believes me.

"We're leaving."

"Yeh."

I look away again, up into the branches of the mango tree, remembering Boima's words, *"an' sweet connec' to dry."* When I turn around, I

163

see that Te Te is kneeling in the grass, a few yards away from the mango tree. She is holding something in her hand.

"What are you doing?" I ask her, edging closer.

"Kpelle way," she says, opening her hand and showing me a small round orange. "Plant the seed and orange tree comin' grow. We do it fo' Boima. To remember."

"Why an orange tree?"

"Orange, that roun', jes' like the sun an' the moon. Jes' like the earth where we livin'. Ehn't you know, livin' that the same to the circle. Everything goin' roun' and roun' an' never stop. That the way o' the world."

"Let's plant it over here," I say, "so when it grows up it can see the mango tree. Boima would like that, I think."

"Yeh."

So we peel the orange together and choose the largest seed for planting. We pour a little water in the soil to help the tiny roots along, but Te Te says things grow so quickly in Liberia that it will not need much help. When we are finished, I wipe the dirt from my hands and look around the yard, at the tall grass and the red flowers along the hibiscus hedge. I hope there will be more rain than usual this year. That way the seedling will sprout and grow so fast that it will rise above the guava bushes and the low-growing papaya. Someday it may even grow beyond the mango tree. I am sure Boima would like that.

This novel is based in part on my memories of living in Liberia as a child in the early 1980s. However, no work is crafted entirely in isolation. I am deeply grateful to the following individuals for sharing their wisdom and expertise: Susan P. Bloom, Lucretia C. Dennis, Mary Lacabanne, Ruthie Laurence, Deborah Noel, Karyn Panitch, Marcia Rautenstrauch, Masha Rudman, and Garmai Tokpah. Special thanks to John Victor Singler for his analysis of the Liberian English dialect; to Steven DeMaio, who spent countless hours reviewing and discussing drafts with me; and to Michael Deitcher, whose tolerance, I believe, is unsurpassed.

—A. B. Z.